CUTTER

CUTTER

LAURA CRUM

ST. MARTIN'S PRESS NEW YORK

Design by Basha Zapatka

Library of Congress Cataloging-in-Publication Data
Crum, Laura.
Cutter / Laura Crum.
p. cm.
"A Thomas Dunne book."
ISBN 0-312-10960-1
1. Women veterinarians—United States—Fiction. I. Title.
PS3553.R76C87 1994
813'.54—dc20 94-1118
CIP

First edition: August 1994
10 9 8 7 6 5 4 3 2 1

For Bill, who encouraged me to write and supported me while I did it.

With thanks to:

Wally Evans, who helped with the horses and the stories;
Craig Evans, DVM, all mistakes are mine, not his;
Barclay and Joan Brown, my parents;
Jane Brown, my grandmother;
Todd Brown, my uncle;
Dr. William Harmon, my shrink;
and Ruth Cohen, my agent.

All of these people helped me in important ways and I'm deeply grateful.

All the people in this story are imaginary and are meant to bear no resemblance to anyone, living or dead.

Santa Cruz is a real city, as are Watsonville and Salinas, but I have mixed the names of actual streets and restaurants, etc., with fictitious ones, and the book is not intended as an accurate road map of the area.

And finally, since this is a mystery, a certain amount of skullduggery must take place, but I want to go on record as saying that all the cutting horse people I've known have been honest, good-hearted, and hardworking, and none of the incidents described in this book ever took place, to my knowledge.

CUTTER

ONE

The phone jerked me awake at seven o'clock on Saturday morning. Fumbling on the bedside table, I wondered who in the hell could be calling me at this hour on my day off.

"Yes?"

"Gail, it's Casey. Casey Brooks. Half the horses in my barn are colicked. Two are dead already and Jim's off on another call. Can you come?"

"I'll be right there."

The stress in Casey's voice, as much as his words, galvanized me out of bed as if I'd been stuck with an electric cattle prod. Jim was my boss—and officially on call today—but an emergency of such catastrophic proportions shattered my resentment at having my free time interrupted. Grabbing a baggy blue sweatshirt, I pulled on some jeans and boots and glanced in the mirror as I went by. My shoulder-length dark hair bounced and waved wildly in an effect a punk-rock star might have envied, but there wasn't time to fix it now. I slammed out of the house, jumped in my truck, and pulled out of my driveway with a slight chirp of tires on pavement, my mind on Casey Brooks.

I'd met Casey about a year ago, shortly after I'd moved back to my hometown of Santa Cruz, California, to take my first job as a practicing veterinarian. It had been an encounter of an oddly picturesque intensity; Casey was half hidden in a blur of dust, pushing cattle down a crowding alley; I could just make out the shape of a cowboy hat and hear his yell—"Hoo-aw."

Standing by the arena fence, I'd watched the cattle move slowly down the alley and into the pen. The whooping shape behind them rode out of the cloud—a tall denim-clad figure on a little roan mare. He carried a rope, which he was twirling lazily at the heels of the last few steers, and he looked me over without comment and kept on about his business, pushing the steers into a corner and loping the roan mare back and forth in front of them. He didn't acknowledge me in any way.

Now I'm not unfamiliar with the semihostile, passive-aggressive behavior displayed by some of the good-old-boy types toward women—and I'm not particularly patient with it. After waiting another polite minute for him to stop and greet me and being ignored, I'd opened the arena gate and marched in. When I'd walked far enough that I was actually in his way, he'd pulled his horse up.

"If you're from Will George, you can go to hell." He said it almost pleasantly.

"I don't know what you're talking about," I told him, slightly startled. "I'm from Santa Cruz Equine Practice. I was called out here to see a sick horse. I'm the new vet," I added, as some people didn't tend to assume it.

He'd stared at me from under the brim of his hat, his face showing an emotion that was hard to place. It was a mobile, expressive face—the features were nondescript and unremarkable, like his brown eyes and hair, but the sense of intensity that came from him was palpable. I couldn't imagine what was going through his mind.

"You're not from Will," he said finally.

I shook my head, still mystified, but before I could speak he went on. "The son of a bitch is trying to put me out of business." Then he looked straight at me and his face changed. Instantly he was laughing. "You're the new vet?" A long wolf whistle. "Best looking vet I ever saw."

I had to smile. His laugh was so goofy-sounding it was infectious. "Yeah, I'm the vet. Gail McCarthy. And you're . . . ?"

"Casey Brooks." And he held out his hand.

Casey Brooks had turned out to be an original. He trained cowhorses, I'd discovered, but that was only part of what I thought of as his mystique. In some deep, quintessential sense, Casey was that legendary being—the trail-driving cowboy of the old West.

I'd been around the western horse world, at least in a peripheral way, ever since I'd done my graduate work at U.C. Davis, near Sacramento in California's Central Valley—an area where Wrangler jeans and cowboy hats are the height of style. Cutting horse trainers and bridle horse trainers, team ropers and plain old ranch cowboys are still a dime a dozen in the Central Valley, and I'd known plenty of them, but Casey was different. In his entirely independent, oddly fearless spirit I recognized something of which John Wayne was but a Hollywood version; Casey, unlike most men who sported a cowboy hat, neither admired nor evoked nor imitated an image: he was its essence.

Despite or maybe because of his sometimes awkward disregard for conventional politeness, Casey and I had gone on to become friends. He'd been instrumental in helping me to acquire my horse, Gunner, a three-year-old Quarter Horse gelding, royally bred to be a champion cowhorse, who'd been given to me when he severed a suspensory tendon. The owner, a client of Casey's, had been all for putting the horse down; between us Casey and I had convinced him to give the colt to me to be (hopefully) rested into a full recovery. That was six months ago now, and at some point in the interim I'd given Casey my home phone number, which was why he'd been able to reach me this morning. Normally my day off was sacred, but this, this sounded like a full-blown disaster.

Half of his horses were colicked. That meant ten or so horses had gotten sick all at once. Colic is a generic term for any sort of digestive disturbance in a horse, and there were dozens of possible causes, but it was unusual for a whole barn full of horses to get sick at the same time. Moldy hay, I speculated, or the water system had failed.

Rolling the window down, I let the crisp, cool early morning air pour into the truck. It was late September and we'd been going through an Indian summer—sunny days that were much warmer than the real California coastal summer, which is often foggy and cold.

Wind ruffled my already wildly tangled hair as I admired the clear blue curve of the Monterey Bay, spread out before me from my vantage point on Highway 1, half way between Santa Cruz and Watsonville. Santa Cruz sits up at the northern cusp of the bay, a small and still picturesque resort city, though somewhat damaged by the Loma Prieta earthquake of 1989. The area south of Santa Cruz, where I was headed, is mostly rural, dominated by the agriculturally oriented city of Watsonville.

Watsonville has none of Santa Cruz's charm. Set in the middle of the Pajaro Valley, it lacks beaches, wharves, and boardwalks, has few buildings of gingerbread quaintness to interest the vacationer. Though the city suffered equal damage in the 1989 earthquake, there was little agonizing over the destruction of its old structures. Watsonville is a practical, unimaginative town which was built for one purpose—to provide housing and services for the people who farm the fertile Pajaro Valley.

Field after field of vegetables and strawberries blanket that valley and produce uncountable wealth for a few and work for many. Generations of immigrant farm workers have bent over the fields: Chinese, Japanese, Filipinos, and, most recently, Latinos have provided a labor force for the land and brought their varied cultures to Watsonville. Some, particularly the Japanese, have evolved into landowners, but in the main ownership (and wealth) are held by a smallish group of European-derived folks—Italians, Germans, Swiss, Slavonians, a few English.

Indian Gulch Ranch, where I was headed, was owned by one of these old-money land barons, a third-generation Slavonian named Ken Resavich, one of the many "ichs" whose grandparents or great-grandparents came from Yugoslavia and settled in Watsonville. Ken owned and farmed five hundred acres in the Pajaro Valley, primarily raising lettuce and cabbage, and had more money than I'd know what to do with.

Casey Brooks worked for Ken as a resident trainer—Ken's hobby being cowhorses—and was allowed to train other people's horses on the side to supplement his income. It wasn't an uncommon arrangement; few horse trainers could make enough money working on their own to survive the high cost of living on the California coast.

Taking the Spring Valley exit off the freeway, I threaded my way through the shopping centers, gas stations and chain restaurants of Watsonville's suburban sprawl, and headed inland, driving the speed limit. Hills closed in around me, their flanks round and golden with dried grass, the creases filled with dark green live oaks and redwood trees. Patches of flat ground planted in apple orchards whizzed by, and the rushing air smelled of apples and wood smoke, the faint and indescribable fragrance of fall. Not too far to Casey's now.

An elaborate black wrought-iron gate that marked the

drive to Indian Gulch Ranch appeared around the corner, and I made a hard right turn, my tires screeching a little. Taking the gravel driveway at the fastest clip I dared, I roared past the big house that belonged to Ken Resavich, past Casey's mobile home, and pulled up in front of the barn.

Melissa ran out to meet me, her face blotchy and red from crying. Melissa Waters was Casey's girlfriend. She was about ten years younger than me, in her early twenties, and under normal circumstances excessively pretty in a Goldilocks kind of way. Her childlike face, with its round blue eyes and softly pouting mouth, combined with blonde hair that frothed and curled casually over her shoulders, made her look like the prototypical dumb blonde, but her appearance was deceptive. Under a superficial baby-faced sexiness which she put on for reasons I didn't understand, Melissa had a shrewd mind.

She was too upset for any feminine affectations this morning. "Gail, my God, hurry! Reno's down; I think he's dying."

Grabbing my emergency bag, I ran after her. I had a brief glimpse of the concrete-floored breezeway of the barn, immaculate as always, and then I was at the open door to a stall where a brown horse was thrashing frantically on the ground. Casey was in the stall with him, pulling at the lead rope attached to the halter, desperately trying to get the horse up. The pain was too great. The horse's eyes rolled and his body twisted and heaved. Casey jumped out of the way as the horse turned over, metal-shod hooves crashing into the wall of the stall, legs tangling. He lay still for a minute, his sweaty flanks gasping, half stuck.

"Quick, sit on his head," I told Casey.

He was there almost before I could get the words out, immobilizing the horse by pinning its head down. I took the syringe of banamine out of my bag and knelt on the ground, feeling for the horse's jugular vein. I found it, poked the needle in, and depressed the plunger. In seconds the tense muscles under the wet hide relaxed as the pain-killer took effect. After a minute the horse folded his legs under him and heaved himself to his feet, stood there sweaty and trembling, but quiet.

"Is this the worst one?" I asked Casey.

"Right now. Two of them are dead. Five or six more have belly aches, but they haven't gone down like this."

I looked back at the brown horse. "Keep an eye on the rest of them and let me know if anyone looks worse. I want to check this one."

Casey disappeared and I began checking the horse's vital signs. His pulse and respiration were severely elevated—not good. On a hunch, I took a stomach tap—inserting the long needle into his abdomen and withdrawing fluid. It was green and murky, a sure indicator that his intestines had ruptured.

Casey and Melissa were back in the stall and I shook my head at them. "This one's got a ruptured gut. We'll have to put him down. I'm sorry."

Melissa's face seemed to crumple, and she turned and walked out of the stall quickly. Casey looked after her. "She liked this horse," he said briefly. Then back at me. "Let's get it over with."

I injected the kill shot in the horse's jugular vein and he stiffened, a sudden alarm in his eyes almost instantly superseded by blankness, and I jumped back from his lurching body as he went down quickly, collapsing onto the ground. When he lay quietly on the clean shavings, I turned away, feeling the usual mix of sadness and half-unconscious anger. "Let's go look at the rest of them."

We went from stall to stall, and I treated seven horses in degrees of distress that ranged from mild discomfort to pain almost as severe as that of the horse I'd had to put down.

I did an abdominal tap on this horse, too, but the fluid was clear and pale; the horse's intestines were probably still intact.

In general, the treatment was the same. After checking the vital signs, I gave each horse a painkilling shot, ran a tube through its nose and down its throat and pumped mineral oil into the stomach (to move whatever had disturbed the digestive system along more quickly and loosen up any big impactions), and promised to come back that afternoon and check on things.

Melissa walked up as I was standing outside the barn with Casey. Her face was pale, with red rims around the eyes, but composed. I looked at her, then back at Casey. "So what happened here, you guys? You have any idea?"

Casey's brown eyes were hard, all the changeable, lighthearted laughter that was his trademark gone for the moment. "I got up a little late this morning, went down to feed, and found everything like this. Two horses dead and a bunch of them sick."

"Did they get fed the same as usual last night?"

"Yep. I fed them myself. Nothing was any different."

"No moldy hay?"

Casey gave me a direct look. "I fed them myself. The hay was fine."

I had to believe him. For all his quirky playfulness, Casey was a successful professional horse trainer. He knew the risks inherent in bad hay.

"Your water system okay?" I asked him.

"First thing I checked. They all had water."

Lack of water or bad hay were the only things I could think of that could cause a whole barn full of horses to colic. I shook my head. "It doesn't make sense."

"I know it doesn't. I've been thinking about it." Casey's glance shifted to Melissa. Her eyes were on the ground and she didn't respond. He turned back to me. "Somebody gave them something."

"You mean they were poisoned?" I must have sounded as incredulous as I felt.

Casey's chameleonlike face was angrier than I'd ever seen it. His mouth tightened. "By Will George," he said grimly.

TWO

Melissa's eyes flashed up at that. She was a short girl, and Casey was a rangy six-foot-something, but she looked a match for him as she stared fiercely up into his face. I felt like I had a front-row seat for some intense psychological drama. Unfortunately I didn't know what the play was about.

"Who's Will George?" I asked. That was the name Casey had used the day I met him, I remembered. It had a familiar ring, and they both seemed to expect me to recognize it, but I didn't.

It was Melissa who finally answered. "Will George is the most famous cowhorse trainer in California. He's won all the big events, made lots of money, has the most clients. He's dominated the business for years."

"Why would he want to poison Casey's horses?"

There was some more silence. When Melissa spoke, she seemed to pick her words carefully. "Casey doesn't get along with Will. Will expects the younger trainers to respect him . . ."

"Will expects everybody to kiss his ass," Casey broke in.

He gave a short unamused laugh. "I don't kiss anybody's ass. I don't need to. I can beat the sons of bitches."

Melissa shrugged. "He can, a lot of the time. Will resents it that Casey won't play the game. The cowhorse business is pretty political, you know. You scratch my back, I'll scratch yours. Will's used to other people playing ball with him."

"That doesn't sound like a reason to poison ten horses," I said mildly.

"There's more to it than that." Melissa glanced at Casey, but he was looking away, his face stony. "There was Gus."

"Who's Gus?" I asked, feeling lost again.

"Gus is a horse. The best horse Casey's ever had. Ken bought him last year as a two-year-old, and he was really great. Casey thought he was a sure shot to win the West Coast Futurity. Then Ken sold him to some client of Will's; we never really knew why. Maybe they just offered more money than Ken could turn down. They came and got him . . . it must be a year ago now."

Casey looked at me. "They came to get him the first day I met you. I thought you were from Will."

Melissa picked up the story. "Casey got in a fight with the guy who did come for the horse . . ."

"And I told him to tell Will to go to hell," Casey interrupted. His face was flushed. "And they didn't like it."

Casey and Melissa were staring at each other again like two cats about to fight. "All this still doesn't sound like a reason to poison ten horses," I told them.

"Will wouldn't poison horses, anyway," Melissa said angrily, her eyes still locked on Casey's. "I know he wouldn't." She sounded completely sure of herself.

"How do you know?" I asked.

There was a long pause. Melissa looked down, then back at me. "I used to work for him," she said finally.

I got the impression there was a lot being left unsaid. I

also got the impression that there might be some question as to whether her loyalties lay with her current boyfriend or former boss. Casey seemed to be thinking the same thing. He was watching her and his eyes were hard and angry.

"And I guess it's just a coincidence that that horse Gail just had to kill was my last shot at going to Reno?"

"God dammit, Casey, of course it is." Melissa looked at me. "We called the horse Reno because he's the other horse we had for the Futurity. He wasn't nearly as good as Gus, but he was entered up there." Melissa's eyes filled with tears.

Mostly to distract her, I asked, "What's the West Coast Futurity?"

Melissa bit her lip and glanced at Casey, but he was staring away from her, obviously unwilling to say anything. She blinked her eyes once and answered steadily enough. "It's *the* big event for three-year-old cutting horses, like the Kentucky Derby's the big event for Thoroughbred racehorses. They have it in Reno, every September. If a trainer can win the Futurity, his reputation is made."

I nodded understandingly. "So losing the Gus horse was a big blow. It doesn't sound like this Will George has any reason to hurt you, though. He's got the horse. Why would he poison your other horses?"

Casey lashed out at that. "Because he's a dirty son of a bitch and he hates my guts. I beat him the last time he showed against me. He probably thinks every colt I've got is as good as Gus."

Casey sounded determined to believe in Will George's guilt. Arguing with him looked like a losing battle, but I gave it one more try. "How could anybody poison the horses with you right here?"

"Melissa and I went out last night and Ken's been gone. Nobody was here at all from seven to midnight. It would have been easy."

"Okay, okay," I waved my hand, "I give up. I'll get some blood samples from the three horses that are dead and send them to the lab. It'll take me a minute."

Turning, I went back into the barn. I drew blood from all three horses, thinking while I did it that this was probably a waste of time. If we knew what poison to look for, that would be one thing, but there was an infinite variety of possibilities, and no one test would cover them all. I decided to have the samples tested for arsenic, oleander and strychnine, which seemed the likeliest candidates to me, then added cantharidin, on the very off chance the hay could be contaminated with a type of poison beetle which is still unknown in California, though not uncommon in the Midwest. While I was at it I examined the hay stack in the three-sided storage barn that adjoined the horse barn, but every bale I saw looked clean—bright green, sweet-smelling alfalfa without a noxious weed in sight.

Back outside, I said good-bye to Casey and Melissa, who were still standing in the driveway. "I'll come back this afternoon. Don't feed those horses any hay, just wheat bran, and call me if any of them looks worse."

Casey nodded. "Sure. Thanks, Gail."

I touched his arm. "I'm sorry, Casey, Melissa."

Melissa gave me a small smile, but she wouldn't look at Casey. I had a feeling the fireworks were going to erupt as soon as I drove out. Getting back in my pickup, I waved quickly at them over my shoulder. Melissa's stance, hands on hips, chin tilted back and up, looked combative to me. Oh well. Not my problem. I pointed the truck down the driveway and my mind skipped back to my own life, which had receded into the background while I was dealing with Casey's horses. My day off, though interrupted, was still at least partly mine. What did I want to do?

The answer was boringly mundane. Clean the house. Do

the grocery shopping and the laundry. Visit my horse. Relax.

Boring to some, not to me. Life as a veterinarian kept me frantically busy; I'd learned to treasure the rare intervals of unscheduled peace, didn't feel the need to be entertained. Though I didn't regret the choice which had set me on the road to veterinary school, I did occasionally long for a little more space and quiet in my life, something I was unlikely to achieve as long as I worked for Jim Leonard.

Glancing in the rearview mirror, I caught my own eye—blue-green iris, black lashes, some faint lines raying out from the corners, brilliantly illuminated by the clear morning sunshine. Damn, I had a lot of wrinkles for thirty-one.

Well, you haven't had such an easy life, I defended myself. What do you expect? Easy enough until my eighteenth year, when both my parents had been killed in a car wreck. Since then it had been a long struggle to turn my childhood dreams of becoming a horse vet into a new security. Between school and the job, I'd earned the lines around my eyes.

Wrinkles add character, anyway. I smiled at the vista of the Monterey Bay spread out before me and felt, on the whole, lucky. I liked my job and I liked being back in my hometown—a stroke of good fortune that had been, getting a job in Santa Cruz. If I could just squeeze everything I needed to do into the days, I wouldn't complain.

As I took the Soquel exit off the freeway and headed home, I reflected that I'd expected to have the whole morning free to do chores. Now I had several hours at best before I needed to go back to Casey's. Zipping up Old San Jose Road toward the distant blue ridgeline of the Santa Cruz Mountains, I admired the sheltered, sunny Soquel Valley, cottonwoods in the creekbed just starting to turn yellow, the shops of the little town particularly pleasing in the gold-tinged fall air. My house was a mile or two outside of town, a redwood-sided cabin in a steep shadowy canyon. Coming around the corner at a good clip, I swung across the road, prepared to pull into my driveway, and almost hit the beat-up pickup that was parked there. I swore, swerved, and parked my truck on the side of the road, giving the faded red Ford in my spot a dirty look.

The owner of the truck was sitting on my porch, obviously waiting for me. He gave me his best guaranteed-to-charm smile as I marched toward my front door and, despite myself, I could feel my annoyance start to evaporate. Bret Boncantini was a piece of my past.

We'd grown up together not too far from this spot on neighboring small farms that were now covered with uniform cheek-by-jowl stucco houses. My parents had raised apples—Bret's, eggs—and he and I had played together during our childhood years. We'd grown apart after my folks had died and I'd changed from a typically rebellious teenager into a suddenly serious adult, but we'd never quite lost track of each other and when I returned to Santa Cruz to work for Jim Leonard I'd discovered Bret working as a horseshoer, and our friendship had sprung back up.

I regarded him now with some apprehension. Handsome in an extravagant Italian way, with olive skin and sun-streaked brown hair, Bret had evolved a lifestyle based on charm and freedom. His unexpected appearance on my doorstep was likely to mean he wanted something.

"Hey, Doc," he grinned at me.

I smiled back, a little unwillingly. That was the thing about Bret. The grin that was in his eyes more than on his mouth always seemed to promise that the world was a fine and entertaining place and that you were the perfect person to appreciate it with him.

"So what's up? I haven't seen you in a month. Deb throw you out?"

Deb was Bret's latest girlfriend, and a great improvement

on all his previous efforts, in my opinion. Bret tended toward pretty blondes with empty heads; Deb was a redhead with plenty of brains and a temper. Bret had moved in with her a month ago and I hadn't seen much of him since.

Widening his eyes, he assumed a rueful expression. "Yeah, she ran into me down at Margaritaville last night while I was chatting up a little girl from San Jose. Deb didn't like it. Told me to move out. So I came to ask you if I could stay with you."

Half exasperated, half amused, I looked at him and shook my head. He gave me his little-boy-caught-with-his-hand-in-the-cookie-jar grin. "Come on, Gail. I've got my sleeping bag. I'll sleep on the couch. I'll help you clean the house, even."

I sighed. His green-brown eyes laughed at me—eyes that said "you and me, we understand things."

"So just how long would you plan on sleeping on the couch?" I was weakening and he knew it.

"A couple of days at the most. Deb'll relent."

"You got a job right now?" That was always an open question. Bret shod horses occasionally, trained colts from time to time, did spells of work at various places. He left town for long periods, and from what I understood he'd been a blackjack dealer in Tahoe, a cowboy on a high desert ranch in Nevada, and a logger up near Yosemite, among other things.

"I'm working for Dan Atkins at his cider warehouse. Regular paycheck."

"Okay. You can sleep on the couch for a couple of days. You've got to buy your own beer, too. No drinking everything in the house and then leaving."

"Would I do that?"

"Yes."

We grinned at each other and I unlocked the door, hearing my dog snuffling on the other side. He bounced stiffly around us in greeting, looking like a geriatric blue-gray coyote with a bobbed tail, and Bret stopped to rub him.

"How's the old man? You're a good old dog, aren't you, Bluey?"

Blue flattened his ears and grunted as happily as if he were a big dumb Labrador instead of a cantankerous Australian Cattle Dog. The coyote appearance was appropriate; Blue was as smart, stubborn, and independent as the dingoes he was descended from. It always surprised me that he acted so friendly with Bret; in general Blue was apt to regard human beings with tolerant contempt, as if they were an inferior race in which he was not much interested. He moved away when people tried to pet him; when he was younger he hadn't been quite so tolerant and had been as likely to nip as get out of the way. For whatever reason, though, Blue liked Bret. Maybe he recognized a similar spirit.

After he finished petting the old dog, Bret stood up and gave my living room a quick evaluation. "Want me to vacuum?"

I laughed. "It could use it."

My house was tiny, really more of a cabin than a house, perched on a steep minuscule lot on the bank of Soquel Creek with redwoods and firs towering above it. Bret and Blue and I were enough to crowd the living room, which contained a few pieces of antique furniture I'd inherited from my parents, a battered hide-a-bed couch, and a large Dhurrie rug, patterned in shades of brown and tan. Everything covered with a thin coat of Blue's hair.

"Vacuum's in the closet." I smiled at Bret. No point in being defensive over how I kept, or didn't keep, the house; after all, it was my house. I made the payments, and one of the rewards of the independence I'd cultivated was that I didn't need to justify myself to anyone. "Go ahead and do the floors, if you want. I'm going downstairs to straighten my bedroom."

My stairs were actually a ladder, dropping down through a hole in the floor, space efficient, but occasionally awkward. Downstairs, facing the creek, was my bedroom. Surveying it, I allowed myself for the first time to think consciously about an aspect of Bret's self-invited visit that was nagging at the corner of my mind.

I'd redone the room in the last few weeks, spending a disproportionately high amount of the little spare time and money I had to turn it from what could only be called early-American garage to what it was now. American rustic, maybe.

I'd stripped the pine plank floor and oiled it, painted the walls and ceiling a simple soft white, and left the old-fashioned casement windows looking out on the creek uncurtained, as I liked them. There were only two pieces of furniture, both of which I'd inherited from my parents, but they were so spectacular as to be startling. A huge, rococo antique bed with a headboard and footboard carved in a design of grapevines and wheat sheaves sat at one end of the room and was matched by a marble-topped dresser in the same pattern at the other end. The two rosewood pieces showed to advantage in the plain white room, and their baroque, scrolling lines were matched by a rust and blue oriental rug (my main expense) which lay on the plank floor between them.

Pulling the faded blue quilt up on the bed, I smoothed the flannel sheets with their wild rose pattern and felt deeply satisfied. The room seemed to say things about my inner self that I couldn't. It was severe and yet richly feminine, and I liked the way the watery green light from the creekbed filtered through the windows and played on the rug. And there was no denying I'd created all this partly for Lonny.

Lonny Peterson was a client of mine. He owned Burt and

Pistol, two Quarter Horse geldings he used for team roping, and I'd been called out to treat Burt for a puncture wound in his hock the first week I'd worked for Jim. Lonny's warm smile and quick mind had attracted me, and I liked the affectionate rapport he seemed to have with his horses. I'd sensed a mutual current between us, but nothing had come of it except some enjoyable flirting whenever we ran into each other.

Then, a month ago, he'd brought Pistol into the clinic to be x-rayed for a persistent front-leg lameness; after I'd diagnosed ringbone Lonny asked me out to dinner. I'd accepted, and we'd seen each other several times since, always in a casual way, but the intimacy between us was clearly growing.

As I picked clothes up off the floor and put them in the hamper or closet respectively, depending on whether they were borderline or over the edge, I thought about Lonny, about what I wanted, what I expected. My remodeling of the bedroom had certainly had something to do with my sense that I might soon be inviting him into it. Bret's presence wouldn't be an asset, but presumably he wasn't staying forever. Presumably also, Lonny had a bedroom of his own that he might invite me into.

Vacuuming the rug with the hand-held appliance I kept in the closet, I wondered, as I think everyone does in this era of AIDS, if I really wanted a new sexual partner. Was it worth the risk?

The chemistry between Lonny and me was starting to sparkle, and I genuinely liked the man. But, but, and again but—casual sex wasn't for me, and a relationship, whatever its advantages, had some major disadvantages—not even counting herpes, AIDS, etc. I'd bought my independence at a high price, and I wasn't wholeheartedly eager to give it up. On the other hand . . .

Sighing, I forced my mind off the subject, put a load of

laundry into the apartment-sized stacking washer-dryer behind a screen in the corner of the room, and decided to change out of my less-than-presentable clothes while I was down here.

Replacing my faded Wrangler jeans with some newer Wrangler jeans and my old sweatshirt with a scoop-necked blue-green T-shirt, I brushed my hair, studying myself in the mirror over the old antique dresser. Am I an attractive woman? As usual, I concluded that I'm reasonably attractive, if not beautiful, and I like my looks well enough.

Mixed Irish and German genes have given me a largish nose and a wide mouth, also blue-green eyes under dark brows and skin that tans easily. My unruly hair, somewhere between curls and waves, is Hershey-bar brown or the color of a muddy arena, whichever you prefer. I'm tall (five foot seven) and a little too wide-shouldered and -hipped for conventional beauty; my body looks strong as well as curvy and I'm happy with it, though I'd prefer not to get any bigger.

Confining my hair in a blue-green cuff, I evaluated—neat, casual, a look that said I-work-with-livestock—a look I like. A big-city career woman would probably be aghast. Jeans, boots, and a carefully chosen T-shirt or tailored shirt (flattering color and neckline) are my everyday version of good style, a reflection of the fact that I often end up in a barnyard, no matter where I start out for in the first place.

I applied a little matte-tone sunblock to my face, some blush, some lip gloss—all the make-up I wear on a regular basis—and smiled at the mirror. Good enough.

Back up the ladder, a glance showed that Bret was sacked out on the couch fast asleep, sure that his part of the cleanup was done. Well, the floors were vacuumed. I cleaned the bathroom and the kitchen and checked the cupboard and refrigerator, making a list of what was missing. Snapping my fingers for Blue, I stepped softly past Bret and out the door. After staying up all night hustling women, he probably needed his sleep.

Blue hopped stiffly onto the floorboards of the pickup and I climbed in after him. First the grocery store, and then back to Casey's.

THREE

I pulled up in front of Casey's barn an hour later. Casey was in the arena, working a horse on cattle. No one else was in sight. As I watched, he guided the little blue roan mare he was riding into the herd, reining her gently and quietly, and separated a brindle steer from the bunch. The horse stood between the steer and the safety of the herd, and I could almost see the steer make up his mind to get back. From a standstill he broke hard to the right, then doubled back sharply to the left, diving toward the other cattle. The roan mare moved with him stride for stride, keeping herself between the steer and the herd. Feinting left and right rapidly, the steer tried to confuse the horse, but the mare stayed with him, leaping back and forth, never missing a beat.

It was startlingly, touchingly beautiful. The little horse moved like a dancer—always smooth and in time. Casey sat squarely in the middle of her, still as a statue, his face and eyes intent. The reins swung loose; he left every move to the mare's judgment. Her face was as intent as Casey's, her ears pricked sharply forward in concentration.

The steer paused, unsure what to try next, and Casey

picked up his reins and touched the horse on the neck. She stopped, and all the tension seemed to go out of her body. Casey turned her away from the cattle, patting her on the rump affectionately, and his eyes met mine.

Immediately his wild, happy-go-lucky daredevil's smile flashed on and he whistled, the same long wolf whistle he'd greeted me with when we'd met. "Hey, good-looking," he drawled.

I smiled back at him. "Hi, Casey. How're the horses?"

"They're fine. I kept a close eye on them for a couple of hours, but whatever it was, it's passed off. Have you got the results of those tests yet?"

"Casey, I can't even send the tests in until Monday. It'll be a few days before I know."

His face hardened. Trying to bring back the smile, I said, "I watched you work this mare. She looked great."

Casey shrugged, but the laughter bubbled up in his eyes. "She's a cutter." He stroked the mare's mane lightly.

"What does it take to make one like this?" I asked, thinking of Gunner, my colt, my project, imagining him a finished horse like this mare.

"Lots of time and wet saddle blankets." Casey shrugged again, clearly unwilling or unable to explain any further. His particular brand of intelligence was instinctive; it told him what to do with a horse but didn't lend itself to articulate explanations of what he was doing.

"Want to work her on a cow?" he asked suddenly, as if that were the only explanation possible.

"Uh, well," I stammered, unsure what to say.

All my life I'd been interested in cowhorses—cutting horses, stock horses, roping horses—perhaps a reflection of the American fascination with the cowboy image. I'd owned a retired rope horse when I was a teenager, a good old pony who'd taught me to ride and given me whatever understanding I had of horses and their ways. But life had not arranged itself so that I could pursue my interest; life for many years had been a steady all-consuming struggle to get through vet school, while life at the moment made vet school look easy. I had had neither the time nor the money for cutting horses.

But ride one? Now?

"Won't I just fall off?"

"I don't know. You might." Casey's grin broadened. "Chance you take."

"Will I screw her up?"

"Nah. She's a broke horse. You can't hurt her. Just do what I tell you."

Casey was already getting off, adjusting the stirrups for my legs. What the hell, I thought, you only live once.

"What's her name?" I patted the mare's neck as I started to climb up on her.

"Shiloh. She's a real lady. Wouldn't hurt a flea."

Shiloh seemed taller, once I was on her. The ground looked a long way down. I walked her around the pen, getting used to the feel of her. Casey perched himself on the top rail of the fence, calling out a rapid stream of instructions.

"Just walk her into the herd real easy. I'll tell you which cow to cut, pick you a slow one; you push it away from the others, then drop the reins on her neck and let her alone. She'll do the rest."

Taking a good grip of the saddle horn, I nodded my head, feeling my heart thumping as adrenaline rushed into my blood. Shit. Just hang on, I told myself.

Shiloh stepped toward the herd quietly, her black-tipped ears flicking forward to the cows, tilting back toward me when I moved the reins to guide her. I remembered an old rancher I'd known telling me you could always spot a good horse by the way he "worked his ears."

The cattle glanced up at me as I threaded my way between them; the herd shifted and milled, moving away from the horse.

"Cut right in the middle of them." Casey's voice was disembodied; my eyes were locked on the cattle.

"Push that black one out. Solid black, big steer. Just to your left."

I looked; there he was. Big and black, moving in front of me as I stepped the horse forward. Steer stopped, moved away. I urged Shiloh toward him; he stepped away again. Two more steps and he was well away from the herd, standing in front of me.

Casey's voice. "Just right. Now drop her head."

Obediently, I let the reins fall slack. Shiloh's head dipped down a foot, her ears pointing sharply at the steer; I clutched the saddle horn with white knuckles, holding my breath, and the steer casually trotted two steps to the right. Shiloh flowed with him. There are no other words for it. Riding her was like being a leaf floating on a stream.

The black steer turned back to the left, seeking a way to the herd, and the mare rolled with him effortlessly, a move as sudden and graceful as a perfect turn on skis—the ultimate free ride. Back and forth across the pen we went, staying with the steer, keeping him away from the herd he desired to rejoin, and I felt a wide grin breaking out as I let myself flow into the turns with the mare, feeling the thrill of her timing.

After a dozen or so turns I heard Casey again. "Pull her up, real gentle."

I reached down and picked up the reins and the mare came to an easy stop, her ears flicking back toward me once more as the steer moved away.

"Good girl," I told her, patting the blue roan neck that was slightly damp with sweat, running my fingers through her black mane. "Good girl."

"So what do you think?" Casey's grin was a reflection of my own as I walked Shiloh toward him.

"Wow. That is *fun.*" I got off the mare and patted her once more, saying regretfully, "I'd give a lot to have the time and money to train Gunner to do this."

Casey flipped one shoulder in his characteristic shrug. "I'll train him half-price. For you. He's a good one."

His eyes met mine in a brief glance that said he was serious and I nodded. "Okay. He should be sound enough in another six months. I'll save my money."

Casey was already leading Shiloh away toward the barn and I followed him, wondering if I had just done something incredibly foolish or incredibly smart. I really couldn't afford even half-price training fees. But the feel of the horse moving underneath me, dancing with the cow . . . only one thing I'd known had ever compared to that. Smiling to myself, I thought that was a comparison I wouldn't make to Casey.

By the time I walked into the barn, he had Shiloh unsaddled and was saddling another horse, moving with the restless jerky motions that were typical of him on the ground; it was only on a horse that he acquired that still, poised quiet that was part of his skill. As he pulled the cinch tight on a leggy sorrel gelding he said over his shoulder, "Have a look at those horses will you, Gail? They look all right to me, but since you're here . . ." He was leading the horse away as he spoke. "I need to ride this pig before I quit."

Walking up and down the barn aisle, I stepped into the stalls of the horses I'd treated this morning, taking their pulse and respiration, checking for any abnormal signs. There were none. The poison (if there was a poison, I added to myself) had apparently been something which had caused the horses to have a major digestive disturbance. In some cases their intestines had ruptured from the pressure, which had killed them. In the cases where they hadn't ruptured there seemed to be no further problems once the colic effect had passed. I made a mental note to tell the lab to check for atropine in the blood as well as the other poisons, as atropine was the only drug that struck me as likely to have just that effect.

When I was done I stood in the aisle for a second, hearing the peaceful rustle and stamp of the horses in their stalls, smelling the warm, sweet familiar smell of a barn. This barn had been built by Ken Resavich, the owner of the ranch, a few years ago and was state of the art, in its way. It was a metal building (horses eat wood) with concrete floors, fully enclosed stalls, tack room, feedroom, bathroom, wash rack, office—all immaculate. There was not so much as a stray horsehair or a clod of dirt in the concrete-floored breezeway that ran between the stalls, let alone a pile of manure; two Mexican men were employed full time to keep it that way. The general effect, I thought, was unpleasing—a little too antiseptic-looking. The place smelled like a barn, but it didn't feel like one.

I wandered back outside to lean on the fence and watch Casey.

He had opened the arena gate and was turning the cattle back out into their pasture. The leggy sorrel colt he was riding was high-headed and wild-eyed and danced underneath him with barely contained energy. Casey held the horse with a firm hand while he watched the cattle file out the gate. I watched them too, checking automatically that none were lame, that all looked slick and healthy.

Late afternoon sunshine lit up the round hills of the ranch with just that long slant to it that meant summer had turned into fall. The crossbred cattle fanned out across the holding pasture, their backs deep red and black against the washed-out yellow of the grass. Casey loped the frantic-looking sorrel colt in half circles around them, pushing them toward another gate. I could hear him yelling—the wild "hoo-aw" that was his trademark.

Looking out to the west, where the hills rolled away open and empty toward the blue of the Monterey Bay, dark green oak trees in the ravines, I wished I could afford a ranch like this. Even a ranchette. Somewhere with some space, where I could keep my horse. At the rate I was progressing economically it wouldn't happen until I was about fifty. Practicing as a veterinarian on salary was just managing to pay my bills; even the payments on my definitely low-end cabin were stretching me.

I looked back at Casey and my mouth dropped open. The peaceful, if active, tableau of cowboy, horse, and cattle had broken into a wild scene of disaster. Cattle were scattered in all directions and running through the middle of them, flat out, were Casey and the sorrel colt. The colt's head was stuck straight up in the air, clearly out of control, and he was running blindly. Casey was jerking on the left rein, trying to bring him around, but the horse paid no attention. He tore through the cattle and appeared to be headed straight for a steep hillside, where the ground dropped off abruptly and was littered with boulders.

My hand tightened on the fence rail. There wasn't a thing I could do. Casey and the horse rocketed off the crest of the hill and lunged down in an uneven gallop. Casey still sat firmly in the middle of the horse, and to my complete disbelief, seemed to be able to guide him a little so that he missed the bigger rocks. For a minute I thought he would make it to the bottom and then the colt stumbled and things happened so fast I couldn't follow them.

The colt was tripping and then the saddle lurched sideways and Casey was hurtling off as if catapulted. The horse was down and rolling, and Casey was lying on the ground. I started running toward him, feeling as if I were moving in slow motion.

Casey's figure was crumpled and still; I ran, legs pumping, heart pounding. Casey moved a little—at least he was alive. I ran harder, stumbling on a rock. When I looked up, Casey was getting to his feet. I slowed to a walk.

"Are you all right?" I was close enough to yell.

He limped toward me. "Oh, yeah. Dumb son of a bitch." He looked back over his shoulder at the horse, who was galloping frantically around the lower pasture, apparently unhurt.

I stared at the horse, too. The saddle was hanging under his belly. "What happened, did the cinch break?"

"Must have." Casey was watching the colt gallop. "He's a pig. Tries that runaway shit every other time I ride him. Guess I better go catch him before he cripples himself, though."

He started to limp in that direction and I touched him on the arm. "Save your leg. I'll get the horse."

Casey looked at me and then shrugged. "Okay. He's liable to be a little touchy about that saddle under his belly."

Nodding, I headed off toward the horse. His gallop had slowed to a lope out of pure exhaustion, I supposed. His whole body was wet with sweat and there was foam on his neck. His eyes were still rolling frantically, and periodically he would jump sideways when the saddle under his belly caught him by surprise.

I walked toward him, talking meaninglessly in a calm voice. "You stupid horse, don't you want me to help you, you need to get that saddle off . . . ," etc. I spoke matter-of-factly, my voice telling the horse that things were okay.

He stopped and faced me, his eyes full of fear. He hated the saddle under him, he didn't trust me to help him, but he was also tired and running away hadn't done any good. I saw him hesitate; he thought of running again.

"Whoa," I told him firmly.

He looked back at me, his sides heaving, and I could see in his eyes that he would let me catch him. I walked toward him and took hold of the reins.

The saddle was attached to him by the back cinch and breast collar only, hanging awkwardly and loosely under his belly. Moving slowly, I talked soothingly, and struggled with the buckles, trying to get it off of him. He jumped once or twice, but didn't attempt to bolt with any determination. Eventually I was able to pull the saddle free. Carrying it with my right arm, I led the horse with my left, and headed back toward Casey.

He was already limping in the direction of the barn. I followed him, handing the sorrel colt's reins to him without comment, and slinging the saddle over my shoulder. Casey was walking as if he hurt badly. I wondered if he'd broken some ribs. Something in his remote gaze kept me from asking, though it would have been a natural thing to do. There was, always, a strange tension in Casey; sometimes normal comments or questions sounded odd—superfluous, foolish—in his presence.

He put the sorrel colt in a stall without word.

"Where do you want this saddle?" I asked him.

"I'll take it."

I refrained from offering to help him further, feeling it wouldn't be appreciated, and handed him the saddle. Still limping, he carried it into the tack room and slung it on a rack, stopping suddenly.

"Look at that."

I looked where he was pointing and saw that the off-side billet, a leather strap that attaches the cinch to the saddle on the right-hand side, had torn clean through.

"See that." Casey's voice was tense. "Somebody cut it."

For the second time that day I turned to him with the slack-jawed incredulous expression of a cartoon character. "What do you mean?"

"Look at it. It's been cut."

I peered closer at the billet. The leather had a smooth straight split that ended in a tiny jagged tear.

Casey was still talking. "Somebody cut that son of a bitch up high, under the fender where it wouldn't show. Left a tiny little quarter-inch strip of leather to hold it. I cinch up, no reason I should check the off-side—and the first real stress that billet gives way. Same bastard did this that poisoned the horses."

I was staring at the billet with the slow, cold realization that this was the saddle I'd ridden in to work Shiloh. If she'd made an especially hard turn, if I'd leaned too far . . .

My eyes met Casey's, the shock suddenly personal, and the look in his chilled me. "I'm gonna get that bastard."

Abruptly he turned away, with one of those meteoric mood shifts I'd grown accustomed to. "Come on, I'll buy you a drink."

FOUR

I followed Casey up the hill to his mobile home in silence, still puzzling over the "cut" cinch. Paranoia or fact? I certainly couldn't tell by looking at the leather billet, though Casey seemed to think he could, but two disasters in one day did seem a little odd. Surely life on the ranch wasn't usually this exciting.

Casey was in the kitchen pulling a Budweiser out of the refrigerator when I walked through the door he'd left open behind him. Melissa sat at the kitchen table, drinking a diet soda and painting her nails a sparkly bubble-gum pink. Her "Hi, Gail," was subdued, and she kept her eyes on her nails. Uh-oh.

Casey looked inquiringly at me and held up a beer.

"Sure," I told him. I wasn't crazy about Budweiser, but I liked it a whole lot better than diet soda, and I knew from previous experience that that was all they were likely to have on hand.

Carrying a beer, Casey stomped off to the couch, hiding his limp, I noticed, almost completely. Wondering what prompted such an effort, I picked up my own beer from the table where he'd put it and sat down, taking in the familiar scenery.

Casey's mobile home was furnished innocuously, providing little useful information to the curious visitor. Boring beige carpet and linoleum, beige corduroy furniture, white walls and ceiling. Casey and Melissa had put up no decorations at all and the lack of any sort of taste was so emphatic it was almost a statement of its own. Casey's house reminded me of the barn; everything was neat and of reasonably good quality but completely devoid of any interest or character. It made sense, after all. Both the barn and the mobile home belonged to Ken Resavich.

"What's Ken doing these days?" I asked Casey, searching for a safe subject in what struck me as a touchy atmosphere.

Casey's eyes lost their remote look for a second and he laughed, his old laugh, and cut it short with a wince.

"Making more money. He told me he did real well with his lettuce this year—made another couple of million."

"Sounds simple, doesn't it?"

Casey laughed, briefly this time. "Oh, yeah. Everything Ken touches seems to turn to gold. Speak of the devil."

As we watched, a small white Cadillac pulled into the driveway of the big house up on the hill and a man got out of the car. A short, crisp man in his fifties, with close-cropped gray hair and a conservative light blue shirt tucked into navy blue slacks. He carried a briefcase as he walked to the front door, unlocked it, and let himself in. Ken Resavich in person.

Lights came on in the big house as we stared out the window of Casey's mobile—curtains were drawn. Casey said nothing. I thought about the little I knew of Ken Resavich, which wasn't much, and wondered if Casey liked him, hated him, was indifferent to him. It would have been hard to guess. Casey was a difficult person to read emotionally, and Ken Resavich was even more so. I'd only met Ken a couple of times, but his face had seemed almost wooden—expressionless—though not in any way hostile. I had no idea what he was like, other than he was rich and not an extrovert.

"Ken doesn't look much like a farmer," I said conversationally. "He looks more like a C.E.O., or a colonel in civvies. Was he ever in the army?"

Casey shrugged, his face as blank as his boss' could ever be; something about the inward expression in his eyes made me wonder again if he wasn't hurting pretty badly. I tried a tentative question. "Are you all right?"

"I'm doing fine." His tone was clipped and he took a long swallow of his beer and looked away from me. The message was plain—leave it alone.

Melissa was still painting her nails, ostentatiously absorbed; it didn't take a lot of brains to guess that she was involved in some sort of silent feud with Casey. In fact, all the unspoken vibes in the room were starting to make me feel tense and uncomfortable. No matter what I said it was sure to be wrong.

Finishing my Budweiser quickly, I rose to go. Melissa looked up as I said a brief "Thanks for the beer," to the room in general, and smiled brightly in my direction. Maybe she was trying to let me know it wasn't me she was mad at.

I smiled back. "See you guys later."

I was headed for the door when Casey called after me, "I'm showing that mare tomorrow. Shiloh. In Los Borregos."

It wasn't exactly an invitation, but there was something in his voice that struck me as a request.

"Why don't you come?" Melissa chimed in with another friendly smile. "Casey could use the support."

It sounded as if there were a barb in her words, but Casey

didn't respond, just nodded affirmatively, if laconically, from the living room. "Come on," was all he said.

Melissa insisted on giving me detailed directions before I left, and I took them down, agreeing halfheartedly that I might go.

As I said good-bye and stepped out the door, I wondered how long it would be before Casey told Melissa he'd taken a rugged fall this afternoon—hours, days, maybe never? What *was* going on between them—some kind of a power game in which guilt trips were a weapon?

None of your business, Gail, I reminded myself, as I shut the door behind me. Keep your mind on your own life. My own life, my own horse. Shiloh might be wonderful, but she wasn't mine. I drove back to Soquel, up Old San Jose Road, and turned in Kris Griffith's white-board-lined driveway.

Kris lived about a mile from me as the crow flies, but our two places were a long way further apart than that, economically speaking. Her five-acre parcel was all wide, sunny meadowland, and the big house and barn which sat on a knoll overlooking the creek were brand new—natural wood with a gray stone chimney for the house, white-board-fenced pastures surrounding the barn.

It was the barn I pulled up to, and waving at a glimpsed motion through a house window—Kris or her daughter Jo, no doubt—I headed toward the small corral where Gunner lived, Blue stumping stiffly along behind me, stopping to water trees where necessary.

Gunner's head was over the fence, ears pointed toward me, big white blaze prominent in the late afternoon light, and I smiled when I saw him. "Hey, big horse, how you doing?"

He nickered and stretched his nose out . . . "Pet me, pay attention to me, I'm bored."

"I know, I know," I told him, "it's rough being penned up like this with nothing to do, but it's just the way it has to be for a while." Rubbing his forehead and then the underside of his neck, I explained to him at length that he'd severed both the deep and superficial flexor tendons in his front leg and if he were ever to be sound again, he needed a year of forced rest and inactivity.

He bumped me with his nose impatiently and I held my hand out, showing it was empty. "No apples, no beer, sorry."

Gunner licked my palm hopefully; his favorite treat was beer and I often poured a little in my cupped hand for him, but I hadn't brought any today.

Frustrated, he swung his head in an impatient shake that flipped his thick black mane from one side of his neck to the other. "Well, what good are you then?"—I could almost hear the words.

Smoothing his mane back where it belonged, I regarded him affectionately. Gunner was three years old, a bright bay (red with black mane and tail) with three high white socks, a big blaze and one blue eye and one brown one. Bred to be a champion cowhorse, he'd belonged to one of Casey Brooks' millionaire clients, this guy a dude who'd known nothing about horses. The man had taken his green colt for a ride through the hills one day and Gunner had spooked at a rabbit, dumping the owner on the ground. Frightened, the colt had galloped for the barn and somewhere in his mad scramble for home had overreached with one driving back hoof and severed the suspensory tendons of his left front leg. That was six months ago now, and I could remember the emergency call perfectly.

Yellow light had streamed out of Casey's barn into the soft March evening as I'd walked toward the big bay colt standing on three legs in the aisle. Casey was holding the leadrope, and pain and distress were plain in the horse's eyes.

No trouble with the diagnosis; I'd explained to the

middle-aged, overweight man with the pouting mouth that his horse would have to have the leg wrapped and be kept in a stall for three months, then confined in a small pen for six more, and be gradually legged up a full year later, if he was to have any chance at all.

Whether it was chagrin at being thrown, or natural bad temper, or the non-horseman's unrealistic expectations of what owning a horse would be like, the man had simply shrugged and said, "Put him down." I could still hear the crunch of his expensive Tony Llama cowboy boots on the gravel as he'd marched to his Mercedes and driven away.

Casey'd turned to me, anger on his face. "Dammit, this is a good colt, Gail, one of the best ones I've had. He'll be a hell of a horse someday; that dumb son of a bitch wouldn't know a good one if it bit him."

I was staring at the three-year-old, seeing the quality: legs with good strong bone; long, flat muscles; alert eyes, their contrasting colors combined with his big white blaze giving him a friendly, clownish look, even in the state he was in. And then Gunner, standing on his three good legs, had reached out and bumped my chest with his nose. I rubbed the nose.

Casey's voice had droned on in the background in the timeless litany of horsemen everywhere, "And he's by Mr. Gunsmoke out of a King Fritz mare—bred in the purple, Gail—and he's got a real good mind."

"I'll take him." The words just came out of my mouth as I stroked the bay gelding, and I already knew I wouldn't put him down. Putting down a healthy animal that can be restored to wholeness goes against all my instincts. Besides, I wanted this horse.

"I'll take him," I said again. "Can you make it right with the owner?"

"Sure I can." And Casey grinned. "Hoo-aw, buddy, you got yourself a horse."

Six months later I still had him, and he was recovering nicely. I'd arranged to board him at Kristin Griffith's—both for the convenience and for the fact that Kris was one of my favorite clients and a woman I felt I could be friends with. That was the upside. The downside was that Kris was expensive. Expensive by my standards, anyway. One hundred and twenty-five extra dollars a month was a lot for an underpaid vet to afford.

"Hi, Gail."

I turned to smile a hello at Kris, genuinely pleased as I always was when she found the time to socialize with me for a moment.

A slim, spare woman in her late thirties, Kristin Griffith had the taut body and fine-boned face of a racing greyhound. This, combined with short, no-nonsense blonde hair and her slightly tinted glasses, gave her a stern, schoolteacherish look that both was and wasn't representative of her personality.

Kris was a world-class endurance rider; the genuine toughness that showed in every line of her face and body was reflective of a toughness of spirit that had taken her on to win the hundred-mile Tevis Cup, a legendary race. But the part of her that didn't show on first acquaintance was her playful streak, an essential lightheartedness that separated her from the driven fanaticism of some of her competitors.

"How's your baby doing?" Kris leaned on the fence next to me for a minute and rubbed Gunner under his chin.

"You should know. You see him a lot more often than I do." I sighed—lack of time to spend with Gunner wasn't much of a problem now but it would be in six months, when he was ready for light exercise. "How's Rebel?" I added.

"Great." Kris flashed a wide smile. "Took him out for a little spin this afternoon. Just twenty miles. He's doing great."

I whistled. "Better you than me."

Twenty miles, a major day in the saddle for most experienced horsemen, was a regular exercise ride for an endurance rider like Kris. Where she found the stamina I couldn't imagine.

Giving Gunner a final pat, I wandered back outside with Kris and we surveyed her horse Rebel Cause, ambling up to greet us with a long easy stride—for all the world as though he'd been resting all day instead of trotting and loping twenty miles.

Among endurance horses, Rebby was the exception that proved the rule. Endurance horses are mostly Arabians and half-bred Arabians, with a few mustangs thrown in. Rebby was a registered Quarter Horse, bred for the track, which means mostly Thoroughbred, as far as his background went. A leggy 15.2 hands, and about eleven hundred pounds, he was too tall, too heavy, and of the wrong ethnic group, so to speak, to be a long-distance champion. But he was.

As if she could read my thoughts, Kris said, "It's all heart. This horse has more try than any horse I've had. He wants to go. And he has *no* quit. It's that, and his ability to recover. He's got the quickest recovery rate of any horse I've ever seen."

Rebel thrust his face over the fence at us and I rubbed the white star on his forehead. Like Gunner, Rebby was a friendly horse who always wanted attention.

"You sure wouldn't pick him out of a crowd on his looks," Kris mused.

"Oh, I don't know," I told her, "he's pretty well made."

"But look at that mouth. And his color doesn't take your eye. And he's light-boned."

I shrugged; those things were all true. Rebby had a parrot mouth, an overbite, that was a serious confirmation flaw, his solid dark brown color was both common and not eye-catching, and his slender leg bones were an invitation to unsoundness. "He's got a nice eye, though," I offered, "and I'll bet he cinches real deep."

"He does." Kris grinned. Depth through the heart girth was a good indicator of a horse's capacity. "Don't worry, you don't need to defend him to me. He knows I love him." She patted the gelding's shoulder. "Rebby's got a home."

I smiled and my eye caught the motion of a little gold Porsche as it turned in the driveway. Rick Griffith, Kristin's husband, was home—no doubt from work.

An engineer for some high-tech munitions firm in San Jose's Silicon Valley, Rick worked long hours and got paid big bucks. Thus this property, the house and barn, and the fact that Kris could stay home and ride her horses and take care of her daughter, instead of work. On the other hand . . .

"I'd better be going," I told Kris as I turned toward my pickup. "Got a hot date," I added.

"Who with?"

"Lonny Peterson, you know him?"

Kris shook her head. I wasn't surprised. Team ropers and endurance riders operated in very separate spheres—they weren't likely to have run into each other.

"Don't want to be late," I grinned as I waved good-bye. I waved to Rick, too, as I passed him on the driveway, and he waved back, with a friendly smile.

But it wasn't really potential lateness that had urged me to leave, it was Rick. Or my feelings about him. I wrinkled my nose. Not so much about him. About them.

Rick Griffith was a handsome, confident man with an easy smile—and an underlying arrogance, I added to myself. Usually in a suit and tie and with a briefcase in his hand, he exuded a polite, civilized essence of power. It wasn't anything he said or did particularly—to do him credit, his manners were impeccable—just the sense that he always expected to dominate any situation. I tended to avoid him.

As I drove down the driveway with its white-board-fence-lined meadows, I pondered my reaction to Rick. I knew plenty of men like him and I could deal with them; it was the element of Rick *and* Kris that bothered me here. I both liked and admired Kris as a person, but I didn't admire the way she seemed to kowtow to Rick.

Kowtow? Come on, Gail, I told myself, why shouldn't she be nice to Rick? He's her husband; she probably likes him. But I couldn't rid myself of the impression that she deferred to him, an attitude I thought profoundly unnecessary, given Kris's obvious strength and intelligence.

For all that I envied her the house, barn, and land, as well as the freedom she had to pursue her sport—a freedom composed of both time and money—I wouldn't trade places with her. I was pretty sure I wouldn't, anyway.

FIVE

I was less sure ten minutes later when I walked through my own front door. Bret and Deb were arguing at the kitchen table and Blue yipped and snapped grumpily at my calf when I accidentally stepped on his toe.

Bret's laugh, Blue's yip and Deb's angry "Goddammit, Bret" seemed to blend in a hectic cacophony; my little house, usually a peaceful sanctuary, felt like a zoo.

Soothing Blue down first, I rubbed his ears and told him I hadn't done it on purpose.

Bret was still chuckling. "Did he draw blood?"

I shook my head. "He never does."

Deb was staring at me in astonishment. "Why in the world would you want to own a dog that would bite you?"

Still rubbing Blue's head, I answered the question as honestly as I could. "I like his personality. He's ornery and stubborn and independent and smart as a whip. It's sort of like having a pet coyote. He's interesting."

Deb obviously didn't see anything appealing in an ornery, stubborn, smart dog, so I quit trying to explain. "He's my friend. Hi, Deb," I added.

A tall girl with short, spiky dark red hair that she wore in wildly tousled styles, big green eyes, a slight dusting of freckles, and a figure that could have graced the *Sports Illustrated* swimsuit issue, Deb was normally an outspoken, friendly extrovert. At the moment, she looked mad as hell.

"Hi, Gail." She gave me a stormy smile and turned back to Bret with the air of one writing off a bad investment. "And if you think you can walk back in any old time and keep living rent-free with me while you go out in the evening picking up women, you can think again."

Having fired that off, she sent another apologetic smile and a "see you later" my way and headed for the door without another word or look at Bret.

He watched her go, looking relieved, I noted, not distressed. My heart sank a little. It was a good bet he was going to want to stay for a while.

Settling myself at the table where Deb had been, I counted the bottles in front of him. Four—that would be every beer I had. Bret grinned, guessing what I was thinking. "I'll buy more," he reassured me.

"I won't hold my breath."

"Sure I will. Where've you been?"

"Checking Casey Brooks's horses. A bunch of them colicked this morning. Three of them died."

Bret whistled. "Whew. Three. What happened?"

"We still don't know. Casey thinks they were poisoned."

"Are you kidding?"

"Nope. I've got no idea if he's right, or just paranoid. He got in a pretty bad wreck this afternoon, too, and he thinks someone cut his cinch." Briefly I filled Bret in on the day and finished up, "and he seems to believe some trainer named Will George did it all."

Bret whistled again and shook his head. "Will George? That's hard to believe."

"Do you know him?"

"Not exactly. I know *of* him. Everybody in the cutting horse business knows Will George."

Remembering that one of Bret's longer-running jobs had been a year spent working for a cutting horse trainer in Salinas, I asked him, "So how unlikely is this idea of Casey's?"

"Pretty unlikely, I'd say. From what I know of Will George, that's not something he'd do. And why?"

"Casey seemed to think Will was jealous of him. Afraid that Casey would beat him at some big event . . . the West Coast Futurity, I think."

Bret laughed. "Fat chance. Casey's never placed at the Futurity and Will's won it four out of the last eight times. Will doesn't need to worry about Casey."

"Melissa seemed sure about that, too."

"Melissa knows Will a lot better than I do." Bret grinned.

"How's that?"

"About the time I was working for Jay Holley, she was Will's girlfriend, not Casey's."

"I kind of wondered. What she said was that she used to work for Will."

"She did. She also used to sleep with him, if you can believe the rumors. It was pretty well accepted, though; she was Will's girlfriend of the year."

"Girlfriend of the year?"

"Sure. He tends to come up with a new one every spring, or he did." Bret flashed his grin at me again. "He's married, of course. Has been for thirty years. But it doesn't seem to get in his way any."

"I wonder why his wife puts up with it."

"I wouldn't know. But it sort of goes with the territory. Most trainers are that way; there's exceptions, of course."

I nodded sagely. In my experience, Bret was right. Horse training, though usually ill paid, was in some senses a glamorous profession. Trainers were often surrounded by crowds of admiring young women, horse lovers all, each of whom would be honored to be the trainer's current fling. Not a role I'd relish, myself.

"You know all these people, don't you?" I asked Bret, an idea dawning in my head.

"Sort of. I used to haul Jay's horses to the shows. I pretty much know who all the big guns are or were. My gossip's a little out of date, though; it must be two years since I quit."

"I know what you can do for me," I said slowly, with a meaningful look at the empty beer bottles and the sleeping bag unrolled on my couch, "in lieu of rent. Go to a cutting with me tomorrow."

Bret looked wary, but not terribly resistant. "Where?" he asked cautiously.

"In Los Borregos. Don't worry, I'll drive," I added, knowing that he was calculating the price of gas. "I'm not sure that truck of yours would make it over Pacheco Pass. I just want you to go along and tell me about the people and the cutting. Casey's showing a horse—a horse I rode this afternoon." I explained about Casey and Shiloh.

When I was done, Bret shrugged one shoulder. "Okay—I'll go point out the sights."

I smiled. "You just bought yourself a week of free rent, buddy. After that, we'll see. And you still need to buy your own beer," I amended quickly, seeing the thought pass through his mind before he opened his mouth.

He grinned and got up. "I better get to buying, then. Can't sit here all evening without beer. I'll be back," he added, as he walked toward the front door.

That was debatable. Bret was more than likely to wind up at some bar or succession of bars and be back around 3:00 A.M., if he didn't find a girl to go home with.

"Don't hurry," I called after him as the door closed. "I'm going out."

And soon, I realized; it was time to get moving if I didn't want to be late. I was meeting Lonny at the Bohemian Cafe at six-thirty and it was already five-forty-five.

Choosing one of my few dresses in honor of the warm fall weather, I pulled on a lightweight, pale blue denim affair, sleeveless and scoop-necked, worn over bare legs and woven leather sandals. The dress was younger in style than I was, or felt, but it flattered my figure and my coloring and seemed appropriate to the lovely soft Indian-summer evening, so unusual for the coast. Besides, I thought, pulling my hair high with a couple of combs, judging by the anticipatory flutters I was feeling, my heart was closer to twenty-one than thirty-one.

Arriving at the Bohemian Cafe five minutes early, I was pleased and amused to see that Lonny was even earlier; his Bronco was in the parking lot.

The Bohemian Cafe is not what it sounds like. The name suggests something intimate, continental and sophisticated; in fact, the large, high-ceilinged room with big old-fashioned French-paned windows—actually the dining room of a hotel that dates from stage-stop days—looks simple and countrified. The historic bar reminds me of a movie set for the saloon scene in a Western, and all the furnishings are casually eclectic. Worn Oriental rugs cover the wooden floor in patches, Van Gogh mixes with Charles Russell on the walls, and Victorian lamps argue with saddles hung from the ceiling. It's great.

Lonny was sitting at the bar when I walked in and stood up when he saw me. He wore what I had come to recognize as standard dress clothes for him—pressed jeans, an Oxford-cloth shirt, and clean cowboy boots. As a young man, Lonny's face would no doubt have been called homely; his big nose hooked toward his bony jaw and his rough, craggy features had a suggestion of Abraham Lincoln. At forty-six (we'd gotten to the stage of telling each other our ages), he was growing to look distinguished (I thought), and distinguished or homely, his face was illuminated by a pair of greenish eyes filled with life, humor and intelligence—eyes that seemed to brim over at times with an openhearted zest for living.

Now was one of those times, and I smiled up at him, warmed and charmed as I often was by his enthusiasm. I'm tall for a woman, but Lonny's six-foot-two made me tilt my head back to look him in the eyes. "Hi," I told him.

"Hi." He grinned appreciatively at me. "You look like summer personified. Care for a drink?"

"Sure." I seated myself on a bar stool and looked around with pleasure. The bar at the Bohemian Cafe looked exactly the way a bar was supposed to look—ceiling covered in dollar bills, walls paneled in dark brown wood with trophy heads and the kind of "amusing" signs that bars seem to collect over every square inch of space, bottles ranged in mirrored rows behind the old rosewood bar with its brass rail, and the sort of quiet, restful ambience that more modern bars never seem to have. Late evening sunlight slanted in through a west-facing window and dust motes floated like golden specks in the air. Two other people chatted softly at a table in the corner.

I took a sharp, lime-flavored sip of my vodka gimlet and felt relaxation and contentment wash over me in a rush. Smiling gratefully at Lonny, I said, "Don't you love the cocktail hour?"

His eyes crinkled at the corners as he smiled back. "If it's done right, appreciated, yes."

"Having a drink with somebody, a little conversation, at the point where late afternoon turns into evening—I don't know, it doesn't seem to go into words, but there's something about it."

We both took sips of our drinks in appreciative silence. After a second Lonny asked me, "So what's new?"

I told him about Casey Brooks' barn full of colicked horses, his suspicion of poison, and finished up with the information that I was planning to go to a cutting tomorrow in the Central Valley. I didn't mention that I'd invited Bret to go with me; Lonny knew Bret slightly and always seemed to regard Bret and my relationship with puzzled, if accepting, incomprehension, but I felt a need not to arouse any possible jealousies. Since I wasn't yet sure how involved I planned to get with Lonny, I didn't particularly want to deal with any possessiveness he might feel.

In his turn Lonny told me about a practice roping he'd gone to that afternoon—he was starting to teach me the basics of team roping—and we talked about his two horses, Burt and Pistol. I'd been his veterinarian for a little more than a year now, and had gone on several rides with him since we'd been dating, so the conversation, as long as it stayed on horses, flowed easily.

It was only when we'd finished dinner and were considering coffee and dessert, and he asked me if I'd like to have the coffee at his place, that things got sticky.

An invitation to his place—there were definite implications in that. I'd never been in his house before, our dates had involved meeting at restaurants or riding horses. An invitation to "come up for coffee" was surely an invitation to bed.

It wasn't unreasonable on his part. We'd been dating a month and he'd clearly indicated he wanted to be more involved. I didn't fear a one-night stand and a rejection; it was obvious, I admitted to myself, that I was preparing to be involved with him—just look at the way I'd fixed up my bedroom. The problem was more subtle than that.

"All right," I said lightly, meeting his eyes. "For coffee."

Lonny's house proved to be unique. It was hidden from

his barn, up a steep hill and behind a screen of oak trees, so not only had I never been in it, I'd never even seen it. I don't know what I'd expected, but the house surprised me. It was a round house, a decagon, Lonny told me, the whole place arranged around a central room, which was also round—the hub, as it were.

The room we walked into was a sort of enclosed porch/living room, two stories high, with giant windows looking out at the oak trees. Terra cotta tile floors, natural pine walls and ceiling, and a staircase running up the far side to a balcony that overhung the room all took my eye favorably.

"This is nice," I smiled at Lonny.

"You like it? I designed and built it myself. It's a little different."

"It's terrific."

I sat at the kitchen table and looked around while Lonny made coffee. An open archway led into the round central room, which was carpeted and cozy with books and a desk. Most of the furniture was covered in Navajo patterned fabrics, which reflected the same quiet, Southwestern color scheme as the rest of the house. It was gentle and relaxing—a house to be comfortable in. I had the feeling Lonny had created it as the restful center to an active life.

He handed me coffee in a sand-colored mug and said, "Would you like to sit in the living room?"

I got up and we settled ourselves, as if we'd planned it, on the couch. The coffee was good, fresh ground and strong, and Lonny's shoulder was just touching mine. His face was quiet, almost withdrawn, and I had no idea what was on his mind.

As if he'd read my thoughts, he looked at me and said, "So what are you thinking?"

"That's a loaded question," I warned him.

He looked straight at me. "So, what are you thinking?"

"I'm thinking it looks like we're getting ready to go to bed, and I'm still not sure."

Lonny put his coffee cup down and took mine and put it down, too. His hands, as he turned my face to his, were gentle and demanding at the same time. His mouth met mine tenderly, but not tentatively, and the kiss grew in intensity until we were devouring each other. I swam in his desire, the strength and the warmth of it, in his hands caressing my back and waist.

It didn't take long. Our bodies lit sparks from each other. Lonny ran his hand down my thigh and groaned. Burying his face in my chest, he said softly, "I want you." It was there in his voice, an intensity of feeling both completely male and still vulnerable. He wasn't trying to hide.

My body cried out for him, but my mind was warning me. Wait a minute. Is this what you want? All my reservations raised their heads.

"Lonny, I just don't know."

"Don't know what?"

"Whether this is what I want." I forced myself to sit up. "I mean, let's face it, there's AIDS and everything else out there and, much though I like you, I just don't know you that well. I hardly know anything about you. I don't even know what you do for a living," I said lamely.

"I'm retired. Semiretired, anyway." Lonny grinned and kissed me again, and for some long minutes I sank into the powerful physical tenderness. My arms pulled him to me, and I could feel his body coil, the long, strong muscles over his back tensing.

"Is this what you want?" The tone in his voice was fierce and still gentle.

"I don't know. My body does. My mind wants me to be careful."

There was a long moment of quiet. When he spoke, his voice sounded strained. "As far as AIDS and all that goes,

I don't actually know. I've never been tested. I've never had a symptom and I've never slept with anyone who turned out to have it—as far as I know. In all fairness, though, there is one thing I ought to tell you. I'm married."

He must have felt my body jerk, but he went on steadily. "I've been separated for two years, but I'm not divorced."

I sat up straighter and looked at him. "So what does that mean?"

"I'm not sure. I didn't think it was fair to spring it on you later."

My mind was going double-speed now, catching up to my body and outdistancing it in the stretch. "That *would* have been a shock," I said blankly.

The voice in my head was shouting, Steer clear of this one, Gail; nothing worse than a man with a wife. Stay independent. Don't get hurt. "Maybe we do need to get to know each other a little better," I added.

Lonny didn't say anything. His arm was still around me and I could feel the warmth and solid comfort of him. I wondered if he was regretting his impulse toward honesty.

"All right," he said at last, "let's try. How about you? Are you available?"

"Available?" I hesitated. "Well, I'm free. No entanglements. To be honest, I kind of like it that way."

"You mean you don't want a relationship?"

I snuggled my body more comfortably against him. How could anybody not want this? "It's hard to explain. I do and I don't. I've got a strong sense of independence; I'm uncomfortable *needing* anyone. There're a lot of reasons."

Lonny squeezed me gently and I could feel his free hand playing up and down my arm. It sent corresponding shivers up and down my spine. "So how about us?" he asked me.

I sighed. "I don't know." A picture of Kris and Rick Griffith with their seven-year-old daughter Jo standing between them jumped into my mind; was I so sure I didn't want a life like that with a man I loved and admired? I'd never made a conscious decision to stay solitary; it was more that I'd become self-sufficient out of necessity after my parents had died, and at this point I was accustomed to my independence. Making my own decisions, accommodating no one, was a habit, a habit I wasn't sure I wanted to change. Still, there were evenings when the house could seem very empty, when I drank an extra glass of wine just to hurry the unconscious peace of sleep. I could use a lover—some of the time, anyway.

"If I do start seeing you, what about your wife?"

Lonny's face looked sad. "I don't know. It's a problem. I can't seem to make up my mind to get the divorce. She owns half of everything—this place, my business. I can hardly stand to let it all go."

"Is that the only reason you're not divorced?" I asked gently.

"I'm not sure. We weren't happy for a long time. Eventually she found a boyfriend and moved out. I used to want her back. Hurt pride, mostly, I think." He gave me a rueful smile. "It's been a long two years."

I nodded understandingly. I sympathized with what he was saying, but I still couldn't help wondering if financial ties were all he had to his wife. No two ways about it; a man with a wife was not a good bet.

Disentangling myself gently, I stood up.

"So it's no go." Lonny was still sitting on the couch, looking up at me.

"No, not necessarily. I just need to think about it."

His eyes were looking straight into mine. They were greenish eyes, direct and intent, the most honest-looking eyes I'd ever seen in a man. "I want you, Gail, more than I can remember wanting a woman. I want to love you."

The look that passed between us then was charged enough to ignite wood, let alone flesh. It might have, too, except that a cat exploded into Lonny's lap. That's what it looked like, anyway. A big pinkish beige cat erupted from somewhere, leaping into and then out of Lonny's lap, and fizzed and bounced around the room like an incautiously opened champagne bottle, batting at imaginary opponents, the pupils of his eyes black and quarter-sized.

"Dammit, Sam," Lonny said affectionately, swatting at him when he whizzed by.

I smiled. "Saved by the cat. Another minute and I'd have been dragging you off to bed like a cavewoman."

"I'm willing."

"I know. But it'd better wait. At least for a while." I bent down, kissed him lightly on the lips, and headed for the door. Halfway there I stopped to pet the cat, who bumped against my leg. "Thanks, buddy. I never would have made it without you."

Lonny was still laughing as I shut the door behind me.

SIX

At 6:00 A.M. the next morning I was dressing for the cutting. Acid-washed Wrangler jeans, a loose deep blue T-shirt with a row of little buttons that could be left open at the throat, and my newest cowboy boots, lace-up packers in a gunmetal gray. Studying myself in the mirror, I felt satisfied. The T-shirt made my eyes look bluer than usual, and my figure was trim in the jeans. Hoo-aw, as Casey would say.

Upstairs I found that Bret was already awake; maybe he'd never gone to sleep. He certainly hadn't been back when I'd gotten home. He hadn't dressed up for the cutting, I noticed, his faded jeans and once-bright-red, now-dark-pink polo shirt had seen better days. Despite being slightly bedraggled, he was still handsome. His olive skin and Italian good looks seemed enhanced by old, scruffy clothes, rather than the reverse.

As I made coffee in the kitchen I wondered briefly why Bret held no sexual attraction for me. Too much familiarity, maybe? The certain knowledge that he was of the "love 'em and leave 'em" school, and I had no particular desire to be loved and left. Either way, I thought, as I handed him a cup of coffee and smiled at his sleepy expression, looks weren't the answer. Bret had looks to satisfy the most discriminating.

Driving over the coastal hills that separate the Monterey Bay from the Central Valley, Bret and I were both quiet—the comfortable silence of long acquaintance. My mind was on Lonny—what I wanted from him, what I didn't want. The whole issue was confusing me, I had to admit. If I didn't want Lonny, did I want *anybody* in my life? And if I did want Lonny, did I want to deal with the question of a not-yet-ex-wife?

Shaking my head, as if I could brush away these frustrating problems like gnats, I took in the sunny morning and the bright yellow-gold grassy hills that rolled and tumbled away before us to the valley floor. Everything was open space and blue sky. I sucked in a deep breath and smiled, and Bret met my eyes and smiled back. What the hell, I thought, what the hell. It was good to be alive.

Highway 152 wound its way out of the coastal hills and down to the valley as the fall sunshine warmed up the morning air, softening the sharp acid green of the alfalfa fields, gentling the gray and dusty junkyards, brushing the flat, loud billboards, and tinting the rusting travel trailers and sagging shacks a mellower shade. California's Central Valley slipped by outside the windows of the pickup, looking as good as it ever did.

I'd lived for five years in the Valley when I was doing my graduate work at U.C. Davis, and I knew its moods. Ovenlike in the summer, cold and clammy with tuley fog in the winter, often windy in the spring—a soft, sunny day like this one was exceptional good fortune. Even so, I liked the Valley; it wasn't pretty by anybody's standards, particularly those of someone born and raised in a coastal town like Santa Cruz, but to me it felt familiar and comfortable.

I understood the point behind the alfalfa fields, the grain towers, the Holstein cattle, the almond orchards, the car graveyards. The good straight roads ran like rulers, the towns were bare and simple, and if there wasn't beauty, there was, at least, sense.

An hour later, we were chugging sedately down the palm-tree-lined main street of Los Borregos, a typical Valley town with a slightly shabby, left-behind-in-the-fifties air, and took the turnoff to the fairgrounds where the cutting was to be held.

The truck bumped down a dirty entry road and I pulled into a field that was a parking lot for the day. Trucks and trailers in all colors and sizes were parked every which way on the mowed grass, and horses were everywhere—tied to trailers, nickering to their companions, being ridden at a fast trot toward the arena, led by men and women whose spurs went clink, clink, clink with every step. The men were mostly clean-shaven, their hair short and neat under cowboy hats, their jeans pressed and their shirts crisp. The women wore cowboy hats, too; they mingled with the men indistinguishably, as equals, their waists cinched tight by trophy buckles as large as those of their male counterparts. The whole scene was full of movement, shouted greetings, the thud of hooves on grass, the jingle of bits and spurs. In the bright morning air, it felt like an old-time circus setting up in a field.

Getting out of the truck, we threaded our way through the parked rigs and the loping horses, keeping an eye out for Casey and Melissa. Bret said hi to several cowboys.

"Don't you miss being a part of this?" I asked him, gesturing at the sunny jumble of horses and people.

"Sometimes. It's a lot of work, though. You're just looking at the fun part; you're not seeing all those 5:00 A.M. mornings when your hands and feet get numb, galloping horses in the fog, all those evenings you're so sore it's hard to get to sleep." He grinned. "Taking it all in all, I don't miss it much."

His glance roved through the crowd. "There's Melissa," he pointed.

Sure enough, Melissa was walking toward us, looking like a cowboy's dream in a tight, satiny pink blouse that emphasized her large breasts, a belt with a huge silver buckle around her waist. With her blonde hair curling and frothing around her face and her eyes outlined in several interesting colors, she was a Barbie doll come to life. Not for the first time I wondered why she chose to present herself as a cheap toy; she seemed to have more on the ball than that.

"Hi." Melissa gave us a welcoming smile, and Bret grinned back at her with his guaranteed-to-devastate-'em version.

"Casey's saddling the horses up," Melissa said, specifically to me, though her eyes drifted to Bret. "We're parked over there." She waved a hand at a long aluminum trailer where Casey could be seen swinging a saddle up on a sorrel horse. "I'm on my way for coffee."

In a minute she was disappearing into the crowd, Bret's eyes following her round bottom until it was out of sight.

"Let's go say hi to Casey," I said, breaking his reverie.

"Whew," he shook his head.

"It's hands off as long as I'm around, buddy," I told him firmly. "I'm not up for breaking up a fight."

Bret gave me an undaunted smile. "I'll have to check her out some other time," was all he said.

We started toward Casey's trailer, Bret pointing out people as we passed them. "There's Will George."

Will George proved to be a stocky man in his late fifties with silver gray hair, bright blue eyes and a still-handsome face. He was riding a shiny, gold buckskin stud horse and talking with some men riding next to him; he looked an unlikely villain to me—in fact, he looked disarmingly unlike whatever I had supposed a hotshot national champion trainer to be.

"He's the big deal in the business?" I said curiously to Bret. "He just looks like another cowboy."

Bret smiled. "That's his style. He never goes in for a lot of fancy silver on his saddle, or fancy clothes. But he's a big deal, all right. He's won the West Coast Futurity four times in the last eight years. He's *the* name in the cowhorse business."

I studied Will George some more as he rode by us. You could see it, if you looked carefully. It was in the way his eyes surveyed the cutting calmly, as if the whole thing belonged to him, in the way the other men seemed to defer to him when he spoke. He was the king.

He was a good-looking old fart, too, I reflected. I wondered what kind of vibes would be in the air if he, Melissa and Casey all came face-to-face.

A youngish trainer with all the silver on his saddle Will George lacked reined a gray mare away from the group around Will and rode up to us. "Well, I'll be damned. Bret Boncantini. You here to ask for your job back?"

Bret grinned. "About the time hell freezes over, Jay."

The man who spoke was around Bret's age—late twenties—and had pale, almost colorless blond hair under his cowboy hat and light-colored eyes with an inner hardness at variance with the smile on his angular, fair-skinned face. Laughing, he spurred the gray mare hard in the belly and galloped off, war-whooping at a woman trying to control a fractious bay colt nearby. "Stay with him, honey, stay with him," he hollered.

"That's Jay Holley," Bret explained, "the guy I worked for in Salinas. Don't let him fool you with that goofball routine." He gestured at Jay, who was spurring the gray mare hard enough to cause her to hump her back and crowhop while he fanned her with his chaps, entertaining the crowd. "He's a tough hand, as good as they get. He likes to clown around—it's his routine—but he's dead serious about winning. He went to work for Will George when he was sixteen, started training on his own five years ago, and he's been doing real well. Will more or less sponsored him; everyone calls him Will's protégé. He was a son of a bitch to work for, though."

"Why, he make you actually do something?"

Bret grinned. "Not when I could help it."

By the time we reached the trailer, Casey had already swung up on a little blue roan mare that I recognized as Shiloh, and I stopped to admire the picture they made.

Shiloh was a pretty horse, fine-boned and graceful with a dainty head, and her steely blue-gray color was complemented perfectly by Casey's black chaps and hat. He also wore a bright red shirt and a large glittering trophy buckle, and Shiloh's woven saddle blanket was in shades of gray and black with a red stripe running through it. Her saddle was decorated with a few small silver conchos—enough to look dressy, not flashy.

"Lookin' good." I smiled up at Casey. "We've come to watch you win."

"Hope to." Casey's expression was serious. "I damn sure hope to." His gaze drifted through the horses and riders, checking out his known rivals, sizing up the competition. "Better warm this mare up," he said abruptly, wheeling on the words and trotting away.

Bret's lips twitched as we watched him. "That goddamned Casey is such a go-getter." Bret sounded amused; being a go-getter had never been one of his failings.

Watching Casey lope Shiloh around the warm-up ring, I felt a faint anticipatory tingle in my stomach, a mere shadow, I realized, of what the riders on the cutting horses must be feeling. I wished suddenly that I were out there on

Gunner, getting ready to show him in competition. Maybe someday, I told myself.

Casey's face was still, almost somber, under his black felt hat as he loped; his attitude seemed businesslike and concentrated. I wondered how much inward pain was concealed under that quiet exterior; surely he couldn't be entirely healed from yesterday's fall.

Melissa had returned, carrying two cups of coffee, and was standing next to me. "Casey took off, as usual," she muttered. "Anybody want this coffee?" Her eyes moved to Casey as she spoke, and I saw her face stiffen suddenly. "Oh, no," she breathed, "Martha Welch."

I looked where she was looking and saw a middle-aged woman march into the ring and step directly in Shiloh's path. Without any hesitation she grabbed at the roan mare's bridle, caught it, and jerked the horse to a stop.

The mare's head flew up in the air, Casey, startled, yelled, "What the hell?" and the woman snapped, loud enough that most people in the ring could hear, "God dammit, Casey Brooks, you've gone too far."

SEVEN

Martha Welch was tall and fit and aggressively made-up, with fire-engine red lips and the type of foundation that hides any clue to the skin beneath it. The tautness in the line of her jaw and the hollows in her cheeks looked unnatural, and the many carats of diamonds on her fingers and hanging from her ears seemed out of place in the warmup arena. Her dark hair was lacquered in stiff waves that prohibited any sort of disorder, and she stared up at Casey with formidably angry eyes.

"If you think you can kill my horse and just walk away from it, you're wrong," she announced. "I'll ruin you, I swear I will."

"Looks like you're working on it," Casey snapped back. After his initial surprise, his face had fixed itself into a controlled mask; only his darting, restless eyes gave a clue to his feelings. He reached down and, rather gently, removed his rein from the woman's hand. "I didn't kill your horse, Martha; it's the last thing I wanted to happen." Casey's tone wasn't conciliatory, merely matter-of-fact.

"You didn't ride him, either." Martha Welch was still on

some track of her own. "Just let him stand in the barn and charged me training fees."

"I rode your horse, just like I rode the others. I can't make a silk purse out of a sow's ear." Casey was firm. "I've got to get ready to show; I'll talk to you later. Alone." And he kicked his horse up into a lope, leaving Martha staring after him.

"I'll sue you, you bastard." She said it plainly; thirty people must have heard her. Then she stalked back out the gate.

"The bitch," Melissa hissed.

"Who was *that*?" I asked. Bret's eyes looked amused.

"Martha Welch," Melissa repeated, unnecessarily. "She owned Reno. The horse you had to put down," she added, to me.

"Oh."

"That's not why she's mad, though, the lying old bitch." Melissa sounded furious. "Casey called her last night to tell her the horse had died, and he said he'd swear she sounded relieved. She had that colt insured up the ying yang, and she'll collect more for him that way than she could ever have sold him for. He was a real mediocre horse."

"Maybe she liked him," I said mildly.

"Not her," Melissa snorted. "She barely ever saw him. She paid a bunch of money for him as an unbroken two-year-old—a hot Futurity prospect, or so she thought. He didn't really pan out—he wasn't that talented—which is mostly how it goes. But Martha couldn't buy that. No way could the great Martha Welch have simply picked a dud. It had to be Casey's fault. She blamed him, said he didn't ride the horse enough. She's just a bitch."

Melissa gave me and Bret a small, angry smile. "She doesn't care that the horse is dead. I was the only one who liked that colt; he was real sweet, even if he wasn't a world-beater. She's just trying to make Casey look bad, because she's mad at him. I wouldn't be surprised if she collects the insurance money on that horse, makes a profit, and then sues Casey for more money."

With a toss of her fluffy golden curls, Melissa stomped off toward Casey, and we could see her talking animatedly up at him as he sat on Shiloh. Casey said little and shrugged a lot. After a minute, Melissa turned away, apparently in a huff.

The loudspeaker crackled; the first class was announced. "Come on," I said to Bret. "Let's go over where we can see. I want to watch these horses work."

As we walked toward the arena, Bret asked me, "So what did you think of Mrs. Gotrocks?"

"Mrs. Gotrocks?"

"Old Martha. Haven't you run into her before? She's been involved with show horses in Santa Cruz County for years. She had a horse or two in training with Jay Holley when I worked for him." Bret chuckled. "She's a dandy. Scads and scads of money—she's the heiress to some kind of timber fortune—and she's tighter than a clam with it. She's been through four or five husbands; she doesn't keep them around any longer than she does horse trainers."

"I can see why. She looked fierce. But I'm pretty sure I've never seen her before."

Bret grinned. "She doesn't get along with vets much, either. She's probably had some kind of spat with Jim Leonard years ago, and won't use his office."

I shrugged. "Well, it's no loss; that I can see."

We reached the rail of the show ring and I leaned on the fence to watch the horses work, asking Bret occasional questions. A cutting, I discovered, was, generally speaking, remarkably slow watching. A herd of cattle were brought into the ring and "settled" by four horsemen—that is, the cattle were herded up against one fence and the horsemen rode around them and through them until the cattle got comfortable enough with this that they quit trying to break and run. The whole procedure took ten or fifteen minutes, after which the herd was pronounced ready to work.

Each competitor rode into this herd in turn with two and a half minutes to show what his or her horse could do. The horses were scored between 60 and 80 by a judge who sat in a small elevated booth in the center of the ring. Every horse, Bret explained to me, started out with a 70, to which the judge added and subtracted points as need be.

The rules for scoring were definite in some ways and ambiguous in others. If a horse let a cow get past him and back to the herd it was an automatic five points off—an easy-to-spot mistake, and lethal in terms of the score. But other things were more subtle—a "miss" meant that the horse had gotten slightly off position; a "hot quit" indicated that the rider had pulled his horse off a cow that was still trying to get by him, rather than waiting until the animal was defeated and turned away; "switching a cow" seemed to mean that while the rider was in the process of selecting one cow out of the herd for the horse to work, he first committed to one and then tried to work another. Most important, a horse could not be guided at all when he worked a cow, and the most common mistake appeared to be "bumping" the bit; a rider would stop his horse with the reins, afraid that the horse wouldn't stop with the cow on his own. All these things resulted in points being taken away from the 70 the horse started out with.

Points were added more or less at the judge's discretion, it seemed, though Bret explained that a horse was supposed to be given credit for certain things—a high degree of difficulty in the cow, keeping the animal in the middle of the pen, separating it from the herd quietly, etc.

I watched the horses desultorily when nothing much was going on, intensely when a horse "locked on" to a cow, and took in the whole scene meanwhile. All around us, whenever it veered from the horse that was working, the conversation between cowboy-hatted men and women was of the West Coast Futurity next week—who was going, who wasn't, who had a good horse, who didn't. Will George seemed to be favored to win once again; I wondered if it would be on the horse named Gus that Casey had started.

When Casey and Shiloh were called, I tuned out the talk around me and concentrated on the scene in front of my eyes—a little blue roan mare walking quietly into a herd of cows. Casey guided her until they had a black brockle-face steer standing by itself, separated from the herd. Then Casey dropped the reins so they hung loosely on Shiloh's neck. It was up to the mare.

Driven by the herd instinct, the black steer made a tentative stab at getting back to the group; he ran to the right, then darted back to the left. Shiloh stayed with him, blocking him, stopping when the steer stopped, turning when he turned, running when he ran. The reins swung loose; every judgment was Shiloh's own. The steer paused in the middle of the pen—fenced right and left, right and left again, leaping back and forth, head down. Shiloh mirrored him perfectly, dancing back and forth with him, nose inches from the ground, ears pricked forward. Her eyes were filled with what I could only call delight. This mare, like many good cowhorses, loved to work. Little shivers ran up and down my spine.

The crowd started clapping. I clapped with them; even Bret gave a war whoop. Casey cut a second cow that was a runner, and Shiloh ran and stopped for all she was worth. Dirt clods rattled against the fence as she slid into the ground and jumped out again the other way. The cow kept driving hard, but the mare never weakened, and when the buzzer sounded to indicate the end of the two-and-a-half-minute cutting run, the whole crowd broke into loud applause and the judge marked a 74, easily the highest score all day. Casey was beaming as he rode out of the ring.

I turned to go offer congratulations, and found Casey in the warmup pen, sitting on Shiloh and talking to two men, one of whom I recognized as Ken Resavich. The other I'd never seen before. Casey's expression looked stiff to me.

I approached the group tentatively, not wanting to intrude, but Casey saw me and gave me a wide grin, waving me over.

"Congratulations," I told him. "That was wonderful; I'm sure you won the class."

"It's not over till the fat lady sings," Casey said, but he sounded confident. "Gail, you know Ken Resavich, right? Gail McCarthy; she's our vet."

Ken and I nodded politely at each other, and he smiled a small, formal smile. He looked every inch a businessman in slacks and a lightweight sport jacket; he certainly didn't look like a farmer. I imagined that farming, at his level, involved sitting at a desk and making decisions on which millions of dollars rested. His formality seemed slightly ridiculous here at the cutting, where the uniform was jeans.

The man next to Ken Resavich smiled widely and appraisingly at me, and I smiled politely back, but nobody made a move to introduce us.

Casey was talking to Ken again, and the other man's eyes swung back to the conversation. In his mid-fifties, with a worn-out-looking face, he had red hair that was fading to gray and fair skin deeply lined and blotched by age and weather. The expression in his eyes was somewhere between aggressively friendly and aggressively belligerent.

"Yeah, we need cattle," Casey was saying to Ken Resavich now. Casey's eyes were directed firmly away from the stranger.

Ken's eyes moved over to him, though, and he asked, "Can you bring them this week?"

"Sure, I can bring you cattle this week, buddy." The redheaded man spoke directly to Casey, with an underlying tone I couldn't place.

Casey's eyes flashed at him, but he still didn't say a word.

Ken Resavich, seeming to ignore or be oblivious to all of the undercurrents, said, "Fine. We'll expect twenty fresh head this week."

"Sure thing." The stranger gave Casey a short, almost taunting smile, and turned away. "I'd better be going. Got to get those cattle rounded up for Casey."

He walked off and got into a flashy, two-toned red dual-wheel pickup, one of the fanciest rigs in the field. Melissa strolled up to our little group just as he jockeyed it out of its parking place and drove away.

"Who was that?" I asked her curiously, drawing her aside.

She glanced at the departing pickup and frowned. "That's Dave Allison." Glancing quickly at Casey she whispered, "Casey doesn't like him."

"So I gathered."

"He works for Will George a lot. He's the one that came to pick up Gus that day; he and Casey got in a fight. Ken's been buying cattle from him."

She focused on the conversation between Ken and Casey, which appeared to be about a horse Ken was thinking of buying. I noticed Ken hardly looked at Shiloh, never stroked her shoulder or rubbed her forehead. Wondering what drove him to be in the horse business—he certainly didn't appear to love horses—I wandered off in Bret's direction.

He ambled over to meet me; he'd been chatting with his ex-employer, Jay Holley. "Jay thinks that Shiloh mare is the best novice horse he's seen in years," Bret said as he walked up.

"She sure looked great to me," I agreed, "though I don't

know much about it. Who's Dave Allison?" I asked him curiously.

Bret laughed. "Oh, old Dave. Dave's your classic failed horse trainer. He used to be a big name in the business, so they say. That'd be before my time. The boys tell me he'd let all the horses stand in the barn for weeks and never ride one. Too busy drinking and chasing girls." Bret grinned. Drinking and chasing girls were his normal occupations. "Then, when a show would come along, Dave'd get the horses out and try to tune them up the day before. Eventually people quit sending him horses. He more or less works for Will George these days, I think."

"He works for him?"

"Will gets so many horses he sends the ones he isn't crazy about to other trainers to ride—for half the training fees. That's what Dave is these days—a hired boy for Will. He raises cattle, too. But he did used to be a big name."

"He sure drives a fancy truck."

"The bank probably owns it." Bret grinned his impish grin. "All these trainers are big on keeping up with the Joneses. Every single one of them has to have just as big and fancy of a dually pickup as the next guy, even if they're about to go broke."

I smiled at Bret's irreverence and looked back at the little group surrounding Casey. They were moving in our direction, Casey riding Shiloh and talking to Ken, Melissa following them. Jay Holley rode by and called a comment I didn't catch; Casey responded with a wild "Hoo-aw" and a wide grin.

As I watched, the sound of cheering from the show ring caught my attention. It caught the attention of Casey's group, too, and they all looked in that direction.

The loudspeaker crackled and blared, "Gold Coin, ridden by Will George, marks a 75. As that was our last horse to work, ladies and gentlemen, Will wins the Novice class."

The voice had scarcely finished when Will George rode by us, flanked with chattering acolytes. His handsome face was serene, and he gave me a pleasant, meaningless smile as his eyes moved on to Casey. He smiled again and there was no mistaking it; this time his eyes held a triumphant, gloating expression. He rode on without a word.

I looked at Casey. He was staring after Will George, his emotions plainly readable for once.

"What've you got to do, kill the bastard to beat him?" Casey said it savagely, loud enough for all of us to hear, before wheeling Shiloh and trotting off, ignoring the second place that was being announced as his.

I watched his departing back and felt misgivings. Casey, volatile as a Roman candle, looked as if he might suddenly start showering sparks in all directions, regardless of the consequences.

EIGHT

Monday morning dawned with a more or less routine set of veterinary problems on the schedule. Horseshows and feuding trainers behind me, I forgot Casey Brooks and his troubles except for a brief moment when I mailed the blood samples from his horses off to the lab.

I had plenty else to occupy my mind. A first-class jumping horse with what looked like a bone chip in his knee had to be referred to the veterinary surgery center at Davis, a polo pony with a hind-leg lameness that turned out to be bone spavin—a type of arthritis—required that I reassure his owner for the better part of an hour, then two mild colic cases, and a recheck on a horse with a bowed tendon that hadn't improved as it should . . . by the time I was done, it was well past dinner time.

The rest of the week passed with veterinary problems filling my time, much as usual, and it wasn't until Friday, when the lab tests came back, that Casey was recalled to my mind. I barely had time to look at the results before receiving my first patient of the day—an expensive two-year-old Thoroughbred jumping prospect—a cryptorchid who was scheduled to become a gelding. Removing a testicle that has not descended involves anesthetizing the horse and hooking it up to oxygen, and finding the testicle can be a longish, complicated procedure. I had my hands full, literally, for several hours, and no time to think about Casey.

By the time I'd finished with the colt, now a gelding, it was almost noon, and I decided to run out to Indian Gulch Ranch and stop for a sandwich on the way back. Summer was still hanging on; warm air rushed in through the open window of the truck, feeling almost balmy against my skin. Only the slant of the light, the tinge of yellow in the leaves, an undercurrent of wood fires and ripe fruit gave the game away. October was right around the corner.

Indian Gulch Ranch looked oddly deserted when I pulled up in front of the barn. A quick scan revealed that all the vehicles were gone; Ken's white Cadillac was missing from his driveway and Casey's beige pickup, the only thing I'd ever seen him or Melissa drive, was nowhere in evidence. It looked like my timing was bad.

I'd been sitting there a few minutes, hoping vainly that someone would emerge from the barn or one of the houses, when I noticed the horse standing at the pasture gate. I noticed it because it was a saddled horse. A saddled horse, I realized, that was loose, dragging its bridle reins and occasionally stepping on them as it paced back and forth beside the gate.

The horse was Shiloh, and it was a cinch she wasn't supposed to be running around like that. I got out of the truck and went over to catch her.

The closer I got the more puzzled I got. Casey would never have tied Shiloh up by the bridle reins and left her—that was asking for a broken bridle—therefore, he must have been riding her. Had he gotten off to do something, let go of the reins for a second and lost her?

I studied the hills around me—no Casey, no movement at all but the slight motion of the grass in the breeze.

Shiloh looked at me in friendly greeting; she was clearly relieved when I reached for her reins and didn't try to evade me.

"Hey, girl, what's the matter? Where's Casey?"

Shiloh, naturally, made no answer, and I stared at the plainly marked trail running up the nearest hill toward a ridge in the distance. Was Casey up there somewhere, maybe, God forbid, hurt?

I made a snap decision and, shortening the stirrup leathers to fit my legs, clambered up on Shiloh, who stood docilely for me, like the lady she was.

Clucking to her, I bumped her gently with my heels, and she moved off in a long swinging walk, taking the trail automatically, without my guidance. It was clear she'd been this way often.

We crested one hill, then the next, Shiloh moving surefootedly on a loose rein as I took in the scenery and looked for Casey. Nothing. Just empty hills—washed-out yellow-gold against a deep blue sky—oak trees, an occasional ground squirrel, a flock of quail under some greasewood. High above me a hawk circled, drifting on the currents.

Two or three more hills later and we were climbing the ridge with me wondering if I was on a wild-goose chase. Occasionally I yelled, "Casey," my voice sounding forlorn, quickly swallowed up by the silence.

Shiloh's black-tipped ears moved forward and back, listening to me, looking in the direction of noises. The trail grew steeper, clinging to one side of the hill, and it seemed to me the mare was getting tense, her ears pointing rigidly forward, her eyes staring up the trail.

To my left the hill dropped off into a steep gully, thick with boulders, no doubt the channel of a bouncing stream after a rainfall. Now it was dry—a creekbed full of rocks.

On my right the bank rose sharply, also rocky, with clumps of young oak and brush between the rocks.

We rounded a corner where the hill grew even steeper, and Shiloh came to a dead stop. Her ears were up and I could feel her heart beating in great thuds. She was almost trembling, and I gripped the saddle horn tightly, praying she wouldn't jump off the edge.

Kicking gently with my feet, I urged her, "Come on, girl."

But Shiloh wouldn't move. She snorted, she trembled, and she stuck. It was obvious she would have liked to dive away from whatever was frightening her, but she was too well broke for that. She just refused to go forward.

"Casey," I called tentatively. "Casey."

No answer. After a minute, I slid carefully off Shiloh and wrapped her reins around an oak sapling. It wouldn't stop her if she was determined to leave, but tying her up wouldn't achieve anything; she'd only break the bridle if she pulled back.

"You stay here," I told her.

She cocked an ear at me as if she understood, and she did seem more relaxed, now that I wasn't urging her forward.

Calling out Casey's name, I walked up the trail, around the corner, yelling and scanning the hills. It was red that caught my eye, red down in the gully. Casey's red shirt, I realized a split second later—Casey's or someone's; someone lying still, frighteningly unmoving.

"Casey!" I shouted, panic plain in my voice.

No response from the figure. Scrambling and slithering, clutching at roots and rocks, I made my way down into the gully, my eyes darting to the red shirt and the blue-jean-clad legs of the person, still unmoving.

It was Casey. I stood over him, feeling my heart lurch sickeningly. Everything seemed to blur except the stark reality of Casey's head, Casey's blood. Casey's head had a dent in it, high above the left ear, a baseball-sized crater in the light brown hair, bits of bone and blood showing. Oh God.

Crouching beside him, I took his hand and touched his wrist, feeling for the pulse, muttering snatches of prayer. Don't let this be real. Don't let this happen.

Casey's eyes were closed; his face looked white, waxen—fragile. The blood in the wound, though still damp, was already a little sticky, not wet, not oozing. Congealing. His hand was cool. I could feel no pulse.

Pressing my fingers under his jaw, along the side of his neck, I felt for the artery—nothing. The hole in his skull gaped at me. He's dead, I thought numbly.

I took a deep breath. He was dead. What now?

Get somebody. Get help.

Gently I placed his hand on his stomach, patting it as if tenderness could bring him back to life. "I'll be back," I told him uselessly.

I climbed up the side of the gully blindly; it was only when I was stumbling at a half-run toward Shiloh and saw the alarm in her eyes that I came to my senses a little. No point in scaring off my horse.

Walking up to her quietly, I patted her shoulder, unwrapped the reins, climbed back on her and sent her down the hill, letting her choose the pace.

Once we were off the steep part I kicked her up to a lope, my mind screaming at me that I needed to do something, hurry, now, though nothing I could do would help Casey. Nothing would help Casey ever again.

Finally the barn was in sight and I urged Shiloh to go faster, against all logic. She stretched out eagerly, her black mane floating back to brush my hand, unaware of tragedy, taking only pleasure in the gallop now that the disturbing scent of blood and violence was gone.

I galloped her up to the pasture gate and opened it with

one hand, guiding her with the other, and shut it behind me. The barn still looked deserted; I tethered Shiloh by wrapping her rein around a hitching rail and ran into the office, which was mercifully unlocked.

Dialing 911, I could feel my heart pounding with the adrenaline that was still pumping into my system.

The 911 operator was brisk and competent; ambulances and sheriffs would be on their way; I was to wait for them. I didn't argue. Hanging up the phone, I went back outside thinking that I'd unsaddle Shiloh, and found Melissa doing it.

"Hi, Gail. What're you doing here? And where's Casey?" Melissa's tone was friendly. Her pickup sat by mine in the driveway, where it had certainly not been when I'd galloped for the barn.

"I just got back from the grocery store," she added, following my glance.

"Melissa, I . . ." Oh shit. I'd broken the news about beloved horses that had died or needed to be put down many times, but I'd never had to tell a woman her lover was dead. I tried to keep my voice steady. "I'm sorry, Melissa. Casey's dead."

Melissa looked more disbelieving than grief-stricken. "Casey can't be dead; he was just taking Shiloh for a ride this morning. How could he get hurt? Shiloh's gentle."

She looked at me as if I should know the answer. I shook my head helplessly and touched her arm, not sure what to say.

"What happened?" she demanded insistently.

"I don't know. I found him up in a gully. He'd hit his head on a rock, I think. I just called nine-one-one."

Melissa stared into my face, shock widening her eyes, and something else—suspicion. "Casey's been up to some weird stuff," she muttered, "he must've called about a million people last night. All that stuff about Gus being . . ."

Suddenly she seemed to shut down, as if an inner voice had cautioned her. She looked away from me and I followed her eyes to where a sheriff's car was pulling in the driveway.

"They're here," she said dully.

NINE

The next few hours passed in a long, confusing jumble. I led the sheriffs and paramedics to Casey's body; they pronounced him dead and carried him in on a stretcher. Melissa was questioned briefly; when they found she knew nothing and hadn't been home at the time, they took her address and phone number and said they'd get back to her. I, on the other hand, as the discoverer of the body, was asked to come down to the Sheriffs' Department and make a statement.

Belatedly calling my office and canceling the rest of my appointments for that day with a brief "tell Jim I'll explain later," I got in an official car and was driven down to the Sheriffs' Department. Once there, my escort, a twentyish boy—he seemed like a boy to me, anyway—abandoned me in a bleak little waiting room to sit for another hour or so. All told I had plenty of time to think.

When the door finally opened, it revealed a woman of about my own age, with wavy blonde hair cut in a bob and a wheat-colored linen suit that had all kinds of class. She greeted me with a short nod and settled herself in a chair.

"I'm Detective Ward."

"Dr. McCarthy."

Detective Ward asked me the routine questions—name, address, occupation, how I had known the deceased, how I had happened to be on the scene—questions I expected. I watched her as I talked. Her features were boyish and rounded, the nose snub, the eyes of no particular color. She looked polished and very professional; the cream-colored raw silk blouse, discreet gold jewelry and light but effective make-up added to that impression. Mostly it was her demeanor; her face seemed to carefully contain itself in a quiet mask, her voice held no emotion.

As we talked, I found myself more and more conscious of her slight, almost reflexive glances at the disheveled strands of hair escaping from my braid, and my unfashionably faded and dirt-smudged Wrangler jeans. The chambray blouse I wore was one of my favorites, but there was no denying it looked like a work shirt and had several bloodstains on it. Next to Detective Ward's slick turnout, I looked like an unsophisticated country bumpkin—filthy to boot.

Despite my best intentions, I found this annoying. It was hard to put my finger on it, but Detective Ward had an aura of disdain. "I'm better than you" was communicated in the tone of every word, in the tilt of her head, the way she averted her eyes. It was a kind of defensive arrogance that I'd seen displayed before by some career-oriented women.

Detective Ward was already into a farewell spiel; her routine questions had elicited nothing that interested her. She'd clearly accepted Casey's death as accidental and was thanking me for my help when I interrupted.

"There's something you ought to know. Casey called me out to his place to look at a bunch of colicked horses about a week ago. He said they were poisoned; I didn't believe him at the time."

Detective Ward's face stayed professionally quiet. "Yes?" she queried.

"He was right; they were poisoned," I said bluntly. "I got the results from the lab this morning. I went out there to tell him. I'm wondering if his death could be connected."

Still no readable expression on the detective's face, but I sensed an inward eye roll. She clearly felt poisoned horses were just short of the ridiculous. "Do you *know* these horses were poisoned? Couldn't it have been an accident?"

Patiently I explained about the blood tests and how they had come up positive for atropine and no, it couldn't have been an accident.

"Atropine had to have been introduced artificially into the systems of all three of those horses, probably by injection. The drug would stop the normal processes of the digestive tract, and the result of that would be a whacking great colic. Bellyache," I explained for her benefit. "Those horses that didn't die of the colic recovered and were fine, which is what you'd expect with atropine."

"Why would someone poison these horses?" Detective Ward sounded skeptical.

"Casey thought someone in the horse business was out to get him," I said noncommittally, wondering if I should add that Casey was sure it was Will George.

As it turned out, I had no dilemma; Detective Ward didn't ask who it was. She dismissed my comments with a sniff and began trying to dismiss me once again. "As," she consulted her notes, "Casey Brooks was found in a ravine, where he had obviously been thrown from a horse which later came back to the barn without him, and the cause of his death was a head injury, apparently from one of the many rocks in that ravine, I think we can take it that his death was accidental. Thank you, Dr. McCarthy, for your time."

"Wait a minute," I interrupted again. "Did anybody

explain that the horse that came in without Casey was Shiloh?"

"Shiloh?" Detective Ward looked blank.

"The horse. Shiloh was a broke horse—a very well-trained horse—and Casey was a tremendous hand. A very good rider," I added. "It's unlikely in the extreme that she would have thrown him. Possible, but very, very unlikely."

Detective Ward stared at me. "Are you suggesting someone pushed him off the horse, or lassoed him?" Sarcasm was just a shade away.

I was getting more annoyed. "I'm suggesting this death looks very strange to me. Just a week ago Casey almost got in another bad wreck and he thought someone had cut his cinch."

"His cinch?" The detective clearly didn't want to ask what a cinch was and hurried on. "It seems extremely unlikely to me that this death was anything but accidental, Dr. McCarthy. If we do have any further questions, we'll call you."

I shut my mouth firmly. Detective Ward was obviously uninterested in cut cinches, poisoned horses, hostile trainers and any other weird horsey allegations complicating a nice, simple accidental death. This time I acquiesced in the farewell noises she was making, seething quietly under the surface.

As I got up to go, I let my temper get the better of me, something I'm a little too prone to do. Turning in the doorway, I addressed a parting shot. "I think somebody killed Casey Brooks, Detective. And if you're not interested in who, I am."

TEN

That was dumb, I chastised myself as I shut the door behind me. You have no idea if Casey was murdered or not; you just said that to provoke her, which makes you as big a jerk as she is.

I felt even dumber when Detective Ward followed me out the door and down the hall and requested at the desk that Bob drive me back to my truck. I'd forgotten I had no transportation.

The same baby-faced sheriff drove me back to Indian Gulch Ranch; on the way I thought of Casey. Hardheaded, wild-hearted Casey Brooks, who had never seemed to fit the modern age he was born in, was dead. Casey, who had loved cowhorses solely and completely, who had seemed wholly alive on Shiloh's back, so vital he sparkled. His sometimes abrasive, often entertaining, always unexpected personality was a memorable one, and my life would be dimmer without him.

Casey hadn't wanted to die; I knew that. He'd wanted to show Shiloh, train more horses, maybe find a colt that could be a futurity winner, like the Gus horse he'd lost. Gus

. . . my mind snapped sharply back into focus. What was it Melissa had said—"all that stuff about Gus"? Was it something about Gus that had caused Casey to call "about a million people"? And was it one of those people who had poisoned the horses and (possibly) cut the cinch? And what did all that have to do with the fact that Casey was dead?

Casey was dead. I shivered a little. That was indisputable. And the horses *had* been poisoned; I had the evidence. It created a strange equation. Those things didn't necessarily connect, but . . . My mind leaped to the picture of a stranger sneaking around the dark barn, catching the horses one by one, injecting them with atropine. There was something deeply evil in the image. Only a horseman could have done it; it would have taken some familiarity with horses to catch ten of them and give them all a shot. The thought of a horse person deliberately causing horses to suffer and possibly die in great pain—it boggled my mind. Surely such malice, such indifference, went hand in hand with a human being who could murder.

These thoughts brought others back to mind; by the time the young sheriff dropped me off at Indian Gulch Ranch my brain was bubbling with questions. Relieved to see that Casey's pickup was parked in front of the mobile, I trudged up the hill to talk to Melissa.

She'd dressed herself in black, I found—black jeans, black T-shirt—but the effect was somehow not that of mourning. The T-shirt clung to her prominent curves, her golden hair was gaudier than usual against the dark color, and her eyes were made up with typical fanfare. Though I'd prepared myself to be comforting, it appeared unnecessary. Melissa didn't look grief-stricken; she looked stony.

"I'm sorry about Casey, Melissa," I told her. "Really sorry. I'll miss him."

She nodded her head, her look guarded.

"Can I come in?" I asked, as we were still standing in the doorway.

"Sure." Her tone was indifferent, neither gracious nor hostile.

When we were seated in the living room, I broke the uncomfortable silence. "What did you mean when you said Casey had been up to some 'weird stuff'? All that 'stuff about Gus'?"

Melissa watched me warily. "Oh, just what you know. About the cinch and those horses colicking, and that bullshit about it being Will George. Casey was determined to get Will into trouble."

"How was he planning to do that?"

She thought about it a while; finally her long eyelashes lifted and I could see she'd decided to tell me. "The West Coast Futurity was run this week. Will won."

"I didn't know."

"Most people don't. It's just the cowhorse people who think it's a big deal. Anyway, Will won on Gus, who you know about." She looked at me questioningly and I nodded.

"A friend of Casey's brought him a tape of the futurity yesterday. Casey watched it and started screaming around about the horse on the tape not being Gus. He said it was a ringer."

It took a long moment for those words to sink in. "A ringer?" I repeated stupidly.

Melissa seemed to think I didn't know what a ringer was. "Yes," she explained impatiently. "Some older horse, a well-broke horse that looked like Gus, being run as Gus, as a three-year-old. The West Coast Futurity is for three-year-olds only."

"Could anybody really get away with that?"

"Maybe. If the horse looked right and it had the right papers, probably they could. It's been done before."

"What did you think?" I asked her curiously.

"I couldn't tell about the horse; I didn't know Gus as well as Casey did. But I can tell you one thing; no way would Will George have ridden a ringer."

"How can you be so sure?"

Melissa stared me straight in the eyes. "Listen, Gail. I'm not going to say this twice, and I'm probably not going to say it to anybody else. I'm not really sure why I'm saying it to you. I didn't love Casey. I did love Will—once upon a time. And I knew Will. And Will wouldn't do that."

I stared at her, sitting there in her black T-shirt and jeans on Casey's beige corduroy couch, and wondered what to make of her. The shock of Casey's death seemed to have popped the cork on all that frustrated hostility she'd only been showing in bits and pieces before. Rather than grieving over Casey she appeared openly angry at him.

She must have read my expression, because she hurried on. "Look, I don't expect you to understand, and I'll ask you not to repeat it, but I wasn't with Casey because I loved him."

"Why, then?"

"Because I love the cowhorse business. You might not understand that, either, but my father was a cutting horse trainer—Bill Waters. He raised me; my mother died when I was three. I grew up in this business and I love it. I don't have any talent; when you're raised in a business you know talent when you see it, but I love being around the horses. My dad died when I was sixteen—it was really hard."

I nodded. I understood that—more than she might realize.

"I wanted to stay in the cutting horse business, so I went to work for Will—and to bed with Will. I was in love with him, but I figured out soon enough he wasn't planning to leave his wife for me.

"Casey wanted me. He didn't have a wife and he was

offering me a home and a life in the world I love. I took him up on it. I guess I was a little infatuated with him at first, but it wore off, believe me."

"Why'd you stay?"

"Because he was good with a horse." Melissa laughed—a short, unamused, unfeminine laugh. "That's funny, isn't it? But he was. He was one of the best hands I ever saw, and I've seen some good ones. I thought he could make it to the top, if I could just rub some of the raw edges off of him, teach him you *have* to play the game a little. Fat chance. He never learned." Melissa sounded bitter.

"Do you think someone killed him?"

Her face shut down at that. "I don't know and I'm not guessing. Will didn't, I know that, and Will's the one Casey was so dead set against. I don't know who else it would be."

"Those horses were poisoned, you know," I said mildly. "I got the tests back from the lab."

"Well, if they were, the likeliest candidate is that bitch Martha Welch."

"Why's that?"

"To collect the insurance money on poor, worthless Reno, of course."

"Why would she poison nine other horses?"

"Because she's a bitch," Melissa shrugged.

"Did those horses belong to any one person?" I asked curiously.

"Not really. Two of the ones that died were Ken's. The one you put down was Martha's. The others belonged to various people."

There went one idea. "Was Ken upset about his horses?" I asked her.

"A little. Ken doesn't show upset much." Automatically her eyes looked to the window, to his house, and she stiffened. "Oh, shit."

I followed her glance and saw that Ken's white Cadillac

sat in his driveway; it hadn't been there when I arrived. He must have driven in while we were absorbed in talking.

There was a note of panic in Melissa's voice as she turned to me. "Will you go tell him, Gail, please? I can't handle it. Not now."

She did seem genuinely upset. Don't be churlish, Gail, I told myself. You could do this for her.

"Sure." I hid my reluctance as well as I could. "I'm sorry, Melissa," I added as I got up, though given what she had said, it seemed out of place. "I liked Casey."

Pulling into Ken's driveway a moment later, I parked behind the Cadillac and got out of my truck slowly. I wasn't sure how difficult breaking this news was going to be; searching my mind, I tried to come up with the appropriate words.

Still feeling unsure how to put it, but thinking I'd opt for the slow and careful rather than the blunt, I knocked on the big wooden front door and after a moment it was opened; Ken looked at me questioningly. He was wearing his executive persona, tie and all, I noticed; no immediate kick-off-the-shoes, roll-up-the-shirtsleeves, and flop-on-the-couch routine for Mr. Resavich.

"I'm Gail McCarthy, your vet," I started out, not completely sure he'd recognized me.

"Yes. Is there a problem with the horses?" Ken's voice was stiff and formal, his demeanor expressionless, as usual.

"Not exactly. But I have some bad news for you."

His face showing not alarm, but recognizable apprehension, Ken held the door open politely. "Would you like to come in?"

"Thank you." His formality was catching.

Preceding him into his ranch-style living room and declining his offer of a drink, I took a seat in a leather-covered armchair and looked around curiously. It was all open beams, dark wood, western oil paintings, and wagon-wheel chandeliers, complete with trophy heads hung over the mantelpiece, and several brown leather chairs and couches. All of it looked expensive and had quality, of a sort. It was exactly the house a ranch owner was supposed to have; it might have belonged to any wealthy man with western pretensions.

I removed my gaze from Ken's furniture and brought it back to his face. He had settled himself in a chair that was slightly more than a comfortable conversational distance away and was regarding me almost nervously, as though a youngish woman in his living room was an unusual and uncomfortable event. Had he ever been married, I wondered. Was he divorced, a widower, gay?

"I'm really sorry to have to tell you this," I said awkwardly, "but Casey Brooks was killed today."

Ken's expression didn't change, but it seemed to me he looked grayer. Somberly he stared at me and waited.

"Shiloh came back without Casey and I went looking for him and found him in a ravine. He'd hit his head on a rock, apparently, and it killed him."

Ken was still staring at me; I had no idea what thoughts were going on behind that wooden face and no idea what to say next, either. I stared back at him thinking distractedly that he would be a handsome man, with those high cheekbones and that square chin, if his face had held even a little animation.

"I'm sorry," I said finally, "I know this must be a shock."

What was he thinking? Somehow I was sure he was upset, but whether it was genuine grief, worry that Melissa would sue him—Shiloh *was* his horse—or annoyance at the loss of his trainer, I couldn't tell. Grief seemed unlikely; I just didn't see Ken as being all that attached to Casey.

He cleared his throat after a minute; his voice, when it came, sounded hesitant. "It was an accident, then? Shiloh bucked him off?"

That was interesting. Ken seemed diffident, as though he were willing to accept that explanation, but I wondered if he, like me, considered it unlikely.

"That's what the sheriffs think," I told him. "I called them and they took my statement, as I found his body. They seem pretty sure it was an accident."

His eyes moved quickly to my face, suddenly sharp instead of blank, and I saw, for a second, the keen business mind behind the stiff exterior. "What do you think?" he asked.

"I don't know. I have a hard time believing Shiloh bucked Casey off, but I don't know what else could have happened. Those horses that colicked, you remember?" Ken jerked his chin shortly. "They turned out to have been poisoned, just like Casey thought. With atropine. It makes me wonder."

Another long silence—Ken regarding me with shuttered eyes. Once again I found myself wondering what he was thinking. When the silence had lengthened to an awkward degree and it was apparent he wasn't going to break it, I stood up.

"I'm sorry to be the bearer of such bad news," I told him again. "Melissa's down at the mobile, if you want to talk to her."

Ken stood up with me and escorted me to the front door. "Thank you for letting me know," was his only comment as he held it open for me.

"You're welcome," I answered stiffly—damn, I seemed unable to speak naturally with this man.

Giving him a small, I hoped sympathetic, smile, I headed down his walkway toward my truck, sighing deeply in relief. Ken Resavich, I reflected, could stiffen the very air around him with his rigidity; how in the world had he and Casey gotten along?

ELEVEN

When I got home Bret was sitting at my kitchen table drinking beer. His own beer, I noted; I never bought Coors. There were only two cans in front of him; it was a safe bet he was still relatively sober.

I sat down across from him. "Casey Brooks is dead."

Bret's face mirrored the shock I was still feeling. "How?" he asked.

"They think he fell off a horse and hit his head on a rock, but I'm not so sure. The horse he was riding—that little blue roan mare he showed last Sunday—would never have thrown him on purpose, and Casey wasn't likely just to fall off. I can't help wondering about it."

Bret regarded me even more blankly. "You think someone killed him?"

"I don't know. I'm not *sure* someone killed him. But there are some funny things going on."

"Like what?"

"Like those colicked horses were poisoned. And Casey thought someone cut the billet on his cinch so it would break. Melissa told me something else, too, but I have a hard time believing it."

"What's that?"

"Casey thought the horse that won this year's West Coast Futurity was a ringer."

"You're kidding."

"No, I'm not. That's what she said. Apparently Will George won on that Gus horse I was telling you about, the one Casey trained as a two-year-old. Anyway, Casey saw the tape of the finals and said it wasn't the right horse."

"Whew. That'd be a big deal if it were true."

"A big enough deal to murder for?"

"Could be. But why would Will George need to ride a ringer? He's got the best horses in the state to pick from."

"I can't figure that one out either. Melissa says he wouldn't, but she's sort of pro-Will. And the detective who took my statement wasn't interested in any of this stuff. She thinks Casey was killed in a fall from a horse, period."

"Maybe he was."

"I don't think so. But I don't know where to begin to find out; I don't know any of these people." I looked at Bret. "You do, though. Do you think you could call your old boss and ask him if there was any talk about the horse that won the Futurity—about anything, really?"

"I'll give it a shot, if you want. I can't see how that'll do any harm."

Bret retired to the living room with the phone; I poured myself a glass of chardonnay and sat back down at the table, sipping and thinking. Blue bumped my free hand with his muzzle and I rubbed his ears. After a minute he grunted contentedly and, giving my wrist a ritual lick, stumped over to lie in his preferred corner by the couch. Blue, though he would have died to protect me, had never been much on being petted. A brief acknowledgment of affection was enough for him.

Bret returned to the kitchen and thumped himself down in his chair. "Jay doesn't know much," he announced. "He did say Will had a contract out on Casey."

I almost choked on my wine. "He had a *contract* out on him?"

Bret laughed. "It's not what you're thinking, Gail. Will's got a lot of clout in the business—he's on the board of directors of the national cowhorse association, not to mention he knows every single person who's anybody. Apparently he told all his buddies not to let Casey win unless they had to."

"Unless they had to?" I parroted, feeling stupid.

"Sure." Bret shrugged. "Like that show we watched. Jay said Casey had the Novice class won, no question about it. But the judge, Mike Pottinger, is one of Will's friends. According to Jay, Mike marked Casey high because it would have been too obvious if he didn't. But as soon as someone came along with a run that was anywhere close, he marked that run higher. If the someone happens to be Will George, so much the better."

"Is cutting really that crooked?"

Bret shrugged again. "It depends what you mean by crooked. Cowhorse work is judged, so it's always a matter of someone's opinion—that's one of the reasons I got tired of it. In a big show, like the West Coast Futurity, there'll be several judges—anywhere from two to five. A little cutting like the one we went to, there's only one, so it's easier to cheat. If you call it cheating."

"What else would you call it?"

"I don't know. Nobody with any brains forgets that the showhorse world is pretty political. Casey Brooks wanted to win without playing the game; that's hard to do. See, there's rules for judging a cutting class—a judge can't let just any horse he wants win. If a horse loses a cow, that's it—he's out of it. But if two horses both have clean runs—

they don't make any major mistakes—a judge can mark them a little higher or lower as he pleases. A guy like Will George gets an automatic extra couple of points because of who he is. For Casey to beat him, at least in front of a judge like Mike Pottinger, who's part of Will's gang, Casey has to have a spectacular run, and Will has to make a few big errors. Then Mike has no choice. But if they're even close, Will'll get the call every time."

"I see what you mean. It still seems crooked to me. The guy that judged that show just placed his friends."

Bret grinned. "Jay said he pretty much went with the board of directors. Except for Casey. He had to put Casey up there as far as second, whether Mike liked it or not. Casey was just that good."

Bret and I were silent for a minute, and I knew we were both thinking of Casey Brooks, who would never show another cutting horse again.

"What about the futurity?" I asked finally. "Did Jay know anything about that?"

"No, not really. I didn't like to come out and ask him if the horse that won could be a ringer, you know. He's pretty good friends with Will."

"No, I guess we'd better not do that."

"Jay did say one interesting thing, though. When I told him that Casey was dead he sounded really surprised—said Casey had called him just last night."

"What about?" My detective instincts were prickling.

"About the horse Will rode in the futurity. The horse that won it. Casey wanted to know what Jay knew about that horse."

"So?"

"So Jay said he didn't know anything about him."

"Oh."

I got up and poured myself a little more chardonnay,

ideas flipping around in my mind like balls in a pinball machine.

Bret grinned at me; he was on about his fourth beer. "So what's next, Sherlock?"

I smiled back at him. "I'm going to call for reinforcements."

Carrying my wine into the living room, I picked up the phone and dialed. Lonny answered on the second ring. We'd only spoken once this week, a brief phone call that had been cut off abruptly when I'd been paged with an emergency. But even though the status of our relationship was still in limbo, I felt comfortable enough with him to ask a favor.

After several minutes' worth of recounting the story of Casey's death and the problems surrounding it, I made my pitch.

"I don't know, Gail." Lonny sounded dubious. "I know Will George a little. He's not going to buy me in the role of a wealthy cutting horse owner."

"You know him?"

"Sure."

"Why didn't you tell me?"

"You didn't ask."

Stymied, I stared at the receiver for a minute, then came up with the obvious question. "So, how do you happen to know him?"

"Oh, Will used to rope a little bit, before he got so famous training horses. And he used to take a pack trip every summer."

"A pack trip?"

"Pack into the Sierras on horses and mules. Camp. Fish."

"Right," I said exasperatedly, "I know what a pack trip is. What I don't know is how you connect with that."

"I used to be a packer. I packed Will in a couple of times."

For a second I reflected on how little I really knew about Lonny before my mind went back to the problem at hand.

"Oh. Do you know him well enough he'd remember you?"

"Sure."

The pinballs were settling into their slots. "Would you be willing to go with me tomorrow to visit him? You can introduce me to him as a friend who wants to buy a cutting horse."

"Tomorrow?" Lonny sounded surprised.

"Tomorrow's my day off. It's either that or Sunday, and I'm on call Sunday."

A long silence. "Gail, I'm just not sure about this. What are you hoping to achieve here?"

"I don't know. Find out something, anything, that might let me know if Casey was right. He thought someone was out to get him, and he thought it was Will George. And now he's dead."

"Is it that important to you?"

"Casey was my friend. If he was murdered . . ." I hesitated. I'd never thought of it in just these terms before. "Well, it sounds corny, but I'd want his murderer brought to justice."

Another long pause. "All right. I knew Casey a little. Well enough to like him; I can understand your feeling. You're sure the sheriffs won't look into it?"

"Reasonably sure." I decided not to mention the rippling undercurrents of hostility between Detective Ward and myself; if Lonny thought this was a grudge match, he'd never go with me.

"Okay. I'll introduce you to Will. On one condition."

"What's that?"

"You don't ask me to tell any lies. I'm not comfortable with that."

"Agreed. I'll tell all the lies that need telling. Okay if I pick you up around nine? I've got an errand to run first."

"All right. See you then."

I hung up the phone and met Bret's mischievous eyes. "I'd have gone with you," he teased. "You didn't need to ask the boyfriend."

"I know." I smiled at him. "But I need a little credibility if I'm going to drop in on this hotshot national champion, and I don't think you'd provide it."

"That's for sure." Bret got up, yawned, stretched, and started to amble for the door. "See you in the morning," he grinned at me over his shoulder. "I may not have credibility, but I've got a girl waiting for me."

"Right." I shook my head at his departing back. "Ask her if she'll keep you a while."

TWELVE

At seven the next morning I was on my way to Indian Gulch Ranch. Overnight the weather had changed, and massive dark gray thunderheads were building up over the ocean as I rolled down Highway 1, Blue asleep on the floor next to me. The first storm of the season was coming in.

Winding up the long grade of Spring Valley Road, I climbed into the coastal hills and drove right past Ken Resavich's front gate. A mile further, I came to a wide spot that I remembered, pulled in and got out of the truck.

Wind whipped my hair around my face; sharp and cool, with the promise of rain. Hunching my shoulders a little, I walked to the edge of the bluff and looked down. Just as I'd supposed, Indian Gulch Ranch lay spread out below me as if it were a child's creation, made out of Lincoln Logs. The barn, the house, the mobile, the arena, were all in full view. Also the pasture gate and the trail leading up into the hills—the trail I had followed on Shiloh.

Going back to the truck, I opened the door and called Blue. He gave me a baleful look and didn't move; at thirteen years of age his arthritis was bad enough that a hike on a cold day was no longer his idea of fun.

"Come on," I told him firmly. "You're going to sit in that pickup all day. You need some exercise."

Reluctantly, he clambered out of the truck.

"This won't take long," I reassured him, "if I'm right."

And I was pretty sure I was right as I slithered through the barbed wire fence and held the wires up for Blue to crawl under after me.

Wind blew straight in our faces as we trudged down the hill, blowing the long, dry, yellow wild grass in great bending waves. The sky was getting ominously darker. I shoved my hands into my coat pockets and turned the collar up.

After ten minutes or so of tramping, Blue stumping along behind me, I saw a bluff I thought I recognized. "Come on," I told the old dog, who was regarding me with an exasperated expression, "I think that's it."

Sure enough, from the top of the bluff I was gazing down a steep, rocky hillside, thick with greasewood and young oak trees, to the trail I had ridden up yesterday. Directly below the trail was the gully where Casey's body had been. I could see some yellow tape wrapped around the boulders; the sheriffs had marked the spot.

"You stay here," I told Blue. "This is a little steep for you."

He lay down immediately; he had no problem with resting.

I scrambled down the hill, stopping at various clumps of brush and rock to peer around. The oncoming storm shook the branches of the oak trees around me as I stared into the ravine.

It would be more than possible. There were dozens of hiding places where a person could crouch, perfectly invisible, and watch the trail below. I couldn't find any signs that anyone had been here, but the loose leaf mold probably wouldn't show them, anyway.

"All right," I said out loud. "Let's say someone parks at the pullout, watches the ranch, sees Casey going out for a ride and comes down to ambush him. Now what?"

Crouching behind the closest clump of brush, I pictured myself as a hidden assailant waiting for Casey. Now Casey rides into view. What do I do?

Remembering Detective Ward's sarcastic "lasso him?" I gave it some serious thought, but rejected it as unlikely. Shooting him would be the easiest, but there weren't any bullet holes in his body. Whoever had done this, if someone *had* done it, had wanted it to look like an accident. Glancing at the rocky ground, I thought the solution was obvious. A baseball-sized rock, thrown from any one of dozens of hiding spots less than twenty feet from the trail, would have knocked Casey out nicely. And if that initial throw didn't happen to kill him, which it probably wouldn't, the stunned man's head could be bashed in more or less at the attacker's leisure, and the body then pitched into the ravine to look like an accidental fall. It could work.

Turning, I scrambled back up the hill to Blue. "I've seen enough," I told him. "Let's go."

I picked Lonny up at nine o'clock sharp. Burt and Pistol were still munching their breakfast hay as I drove in; Burt lifted his head and whickered softly.

Smiling, I slowed for a minute to watch them—two big, strong Quarter Horse geldings, typical team roping horses. Burt was a bay, bright red with a black mane and tail and black socks, Pistol a red roan with a flaxen mane and tail and a blaze face. Both of them were honest, hard-trying performers, though very different in personality. Burt was grouchy, Pistol polite but anxious. Lonny had promised to give me some team roping lessons on Burt, who he said was a perfect beginner horse, and I was looking forward to it.

Lonny's house was warmly inviting this stormy morning. The curtains were open and I could see into the living room, Navajo-patterned couch pulled up in front of the fire that crackled in the woodstove. Smoke curled lazily from a metal stovepipe chimney into the cool morning air.

Lonny himself appeared in the doorway, looking the very picture of a gentleman cowboy. He wore Wrangler jeans, cowboy boots, a belt with a trophy buckle and a dark green, carefully pressed brushed-cotton shirt that made his eyes look green as glass. I smiled at him as he got in the pickup.

Blue was still asleep on the passenger-side floor, and he sniffed Lonny's leg, then licked his hand. "That's Blue," I told Lonny, uncertain as to how he would feel about having an old, smelly, and sometimes grouchy Queensland Heeler sitting on his feet.

Lonny merely rubbed Blue's ear and smiled at me. "You've had him a while."

His smile deepened as he took in my appearance and I basked in his appreciative regard. I'd dressed for the occasion in one of my favorite "jeans outfits"—Wranglers, perfectly faded to a medium blue, and a bulky watermelon-colored turtleneck, with my hair pulled up in a watermelon silk cuff and wide gold hoop earrings. A soft, pale gray wool jacket in place of my usual denim coat, and I thought I looked like a potential cutting horse owner.

"Do I fit the image?" I asked Lonny.

"What? Of my girlfriend? You sure do."

"That's not what I meant," I laughed. "Of somebody who might want to buy a cutting horse and learn to cut. Somebody who was talking to Casey Brooks about doing just that before the poor guy was unfortunately killed. Somebody who is now talking to Will George. That's my role."

"Sounds fine to me. If any of this is fine." Lonny's voice got serious. "I'm a little uncomfortable about doing this,

Gail; I think you're barking up the wrong tree even if Casey was murdered. Someone like Will George is not going to poison horses or kill another trainer in order to keep his position. He doesn't need to. He doesn't need to ride ringers, either. And I'll tell you something else. If, and I'm saying if, someone murdered Casey Brooks, the likeliest candidate is the girlfriend."

"Melissa?"

"Is that her name? I've seen her with Casey, but I don't know her at all. Pretty blonde thing. Young. Lots of curves." Lonny grinned.

"That's Melissa," I agreed. "Why would you suspect her?"

But even before he spoke I was answering that question for myself. Melissa and Casey had not exactly had a jolly love affair; Melissa had told me that. I had been struck numerous times lately with the fact that their relationship had seemed more of a pitched battle. Had Melissa just decided to have the last word?

Lonny was talking. "Just read the papers. Most murders are committed by the spouse, or girlfriend or boyfriend, as the case may be. All the emotions that get stirred up in a 'relationship' are probably the most powerful motivation for murder there is."

I smiled at him. "And you want me to get involved with you?"

He grinned back. "We don't *have* to end by murdering each other, you know. There are different possibilities."

"Like what?"

"Like we live together happily ever after."

I gave him a guarded look. "You see that happening much in real life?"

"Occasionally." Lonny refused to be diverted. "We'd have a chance."

"Okay, okay, I'll give it that. There's a chance."

* * *

We drove over Pacheco Pass with storm clouds sailing by on the horizon and the sky a dark and blustery gray. I was glad I'd thrown my rain slicker behind the seat. Will George's horse training operation was in Los Borregos, not far from the cutting I'd gone to last weekend. Lonny directed me once we were near; he'd been to Will's a couple of times in the past.

When I drove in the entrance I felt a mild sense of awe. A wrought-iron gate with a design of a cutting horse and a cow decoratively welded into it hung from massive brick pillars at the entrance to a long driveway, which wound between a dozen or so small paddocks, all fenced in pipe fencing painted white, all planted in permanent, irrigated pasture. The driveway fetched up in front of a brand-new-looking complex that featured a covered arena, an outdoor arena, a large horse barn, a hay barn, a shop, two horse walkers, and a couple of small, neat employee houses. A branch of the driveway, winding off to the left, led to a palatial brick house with a manicured garden and a swimming pool just visible behind a brick wall. Will's house, obviously. Rancho de Los Borregos was owned, I understood, by Will personally.

Lonny and I looked at each other and Lonny whistled softly under his breath. "This place has sure changed since I saw it last. That'd be almost ten years ago now. Old Will is making a lot of money."

"You do the talking," I hissed, feeling suddenly nervous. "You know the guy."

We got out of the truck into the active bustle of a busy training barn on a work day. Horses marched on the moving horse walker and loped around in the outdoor arena, ridden by several youngish people of both sexes. A horse was working a cow out of the herd in the indoor pen and I could see, even at that distance, that the poised, quiet figure on the horse was Will George. Lonny and I walked in his direction, but we were intercepted before we got there.

"Howdy, folks." The man who greeted us wore faded, threadbare jeans and an equally ancient denim jacket; the clothes seemed to match his faded red hair and battered face. I recognized the face. Dave Allison was his name—the man whom Bret had described as a big-name trainer who had come down in the world.

Dave Allison didn't seem disturbed by his fall. He was leading a pinto gelding with one hand and shook Lonny's offered palm with his other, talking in a genial way.

"You all looking for Will?"

"That's right."

"He's in the covered arena." Dave jerked his chin in that direction and grinned. "Training next year's futurity winner. Just go on over there and holler at him."

Lonny nodded and started to move on, but I stopped, pricked by a memory.

"Didn't you bring Casey Brooks some practice cattle this week?" I asked.

The man's eyes shifted to me and he touched the brim of his hat briefly. "I sure did, ma'am."

"Did you know he was killed yesterday?" I asked tentatively.

"I heard that. It's a sad shame. He was a hell of a good hand."

"Did he say anything, uh, unusual, when you brought the cattle?" Jesus, Gail, I thought, that was lame. You'll never make a detective.

Dave Allison's eyes, so enfolded by leathery wrinkles that they were merely bright chips in his crumpled napkin of a face, seemed to focus sharply on me for the first time. "Unusual? Well, I couldn't say that. What did you have in mind?"

"Oh, I don't know." I was stumbling badly. "What day did you bring the cattle?"

"Wednesday, I think it was." The man was definitely curious now, and I couldn't blame him. "I heard old Casey was killed in a fall from a horse. Was there something funny about it?"

"Not that I know of. Well, thanks." I waved an awkward hand at Dave Allison and hurried off to join Lonny, mentally kicking myself with every step.

Why was I so stupid? I'd learned nothing and succeeded only in making this good old boy suspicious.

Looking back at Dave Allison, I watched him jerk on the paint horse's lead rope and cluck to him, leading him toward a waiting horse trailer. "You better get that roan stud out if you think I'm taking him," he shouted at a hurrying female figure who was saddling horses in the barnyard.

Lonny and I walked on. "Do you know him?" I asked.

"Sort of. I know a lot of these trainers that have been around a while. I know who old Dave is, though I doubt he recognized me."

"Did he used to be a big name?"

"I'd say so. I haven't heard of him much lately, though."

I glanced back at Dave Allison again. "Casey didn't like him."

"Why's that?"

"I guess he came to pick up the Gus horse for Will—the one that ended up winning the Futurity—and Casey got in a fight with him. I'm thinking of adding him to my list of suspects."

Lonny laughed. "If you're planning on putting everybody who had a disagreement with Casey on the list, it's going to be a long list."

I nodded ruefully. "I know. Casey could be kind of abrasive."

Lonny was holding the gate of the covered arena open; I

shook myself loose from meanderings on Dave Allison and stepped through, smiling up at him. "Let's go meet the king of the cowboys."

The king was on a little sorrel filly with a neat white star on her forehead, stepping her into a herd of cattle and parting one out in the familiar pattern of cutting. Lonny and I stood still to watch.

The filly was obviously green; from her appearance and Dave Allison's comment about next year's Futurity, I guessed that she was a two-year-old. Her expression was keen, though, and the dainty red ears flicked forward to the cow and back to her rider in a way that reminded me of Shiloh.

Will George pulled her up after a minute and stood still, looking in our direction. The king was awaiting our approach.

He sat on the filly quietly and watched us as we walked toward him, and the little mare watched us, too, her eyes big and round. Man and horse were a living, breathing statue—the American cowboy come to life. It struck me that Will George seemed consciously to court that image—his battered felt cowboy hat and worn work clothes made a subtle statement, meant to contrast, I was sure, with the flashier approach of some of the other trainers. I was reminded suddenly of Casey Brooks. The two men might have disliked each other, but Casey was the rightful successor to Will's legend. Had been, I told myself, had been. And Will wasn't ready to give up his position.

"Lonny Peterson!" Will George's handsome face broke into a wide smile and his blue eyes twinkled with obvious warmth. "So what've you been doing with yourself?"

"Oh, I go to a few ropings now and then." Lonny grinned back and the two men shook hands. "This is Gail McCarthy," Lonny put his hand on my shoulder. "She's thinking of getting involved in the cutting horse business."

I smiled politely at Will and tried to look rich as I felt his eyes go over me appraisingly. It wasn't a lascivious stare exactly, more like the once-over most horsemen will give a horse they've never seen before—a what-am-I-dealing-with-here sort of look.

Will George tipped his hat. "Nice to meet you, ma'am."

The voice and smile were unassuming, but even in the soft-spoken greeting I could feel the force of his confidence.

"You interested in buying a horse?" Will George's eyes were quietly detached; he didn't need to solicit business.

"I think so. Casey Brooks was helping me, but he died yesterday." I raised my eyes to his face in what I hoped appeared a naive, appealing look, not the scrutinizing study it really was.

It was a wasted effort. Will George's face showed nothing—no surprise, no nervousness, no grief. He said merely, "I heard about that. Jay Holley called me. Too bad. Casey was a good hand."

Lonny and I murmured agreement, and I wondered if it would be carved on Casey's tombstone—"HE WAS A GOOD HAND." It certainly seemed to be the epitaph most people gave him.

"I heard you won the West Coast Futurity last week," I said to Will, naively, I hoped, once again. "Congratulations."

"Thank you. I had a good horse," he said modestly.

"I heard Casey Brooks trained him as a two-year-old."

My eyes were locked on his, but Will George didn't seem alarmed. "He did, that's right. Did a good job, too." He smiled down at me from his horse—a pleasant, relaxed smile.

Inwardly my spirits slumped. This wasn't going to be as easy as I'd hoped. I'm not sure what I'd expected—some reaction to the mention of Casey, or the Futurity, or the fact that Casey had trained Gus, maybe. Whatever it was,

I wasn't getting it, and I could hardly haul off and ask Will George if he'd ridden a ringer.

As he toured us around his place for the next hour, pointing out horses I might be interested in and telling Lonny his program and charges for starting a colt, I gnashed my teeth silently. This was all proving to be a waste of time.

"Is Gus here?" I asked in a last-ditch effort as we walked down an immaculate barn aisle reminiscent of Ken Resavich's.

"Gus?" Will George sounded indifferent. "Who's Gus?"

"The horse that won the Futurity," I said in some confusion. "That's what Casey told me his name was."

"Oh." Will smiled briefly. "He may have called him that. His name's Smokin' Wizard. I just called him 'Bay.' "

How imaginative. No doubt the horse was a bay; it was a typical cowboy mannerism to refer to horses by their color rather than giving them names—Bay, Sorrelly, Yellow, Brownie, etc.

Will was still talking. "He's in that end stall."

We all paused to admire the bay colt standing in the stall; a common enough looking horse, I noticed, and solid bay, not a white hair on him. Medium sized, medium boned, no dished face or Roman nose—nothing to distinguish him from the multitudes of other solid bay horses in the world. I would have had a hard time telling him from Burt, at a distance of fifty feet. He was a little smaller, a little more refined in the head, not something that would be easy to spot from a distance. That lent some credence to the idea of a ringer. A horse with unusual or distinctive markings would be an unlikely candidate for such a scam.

I smiled innocently at Will George. "Can I pet him?"

Will shrugged. "Sure. He's gentle."

I stepped in the stall with the horse, stroked his neck and face, and, trying not to appear too obvious, looked in his mouth. Normal three-year-old teeth—some baby teeth, some adult teeth—as I had more than half expected.

"So is he three?" Will George's voice was amused. He'd noticed me mouthing the horse, naturally; it was impossible to conceal. He didn't sound the least concerned, though.

"Three years old," I agreed.

We all walked out into the barnyard, where a blast of incoming stormy wind, spitting scattered drops of rain, brought our interview to an end. I wrapped my coat more closely around my body and Will George glanced up at the heavy, ominous sky and said, "I'd better start getting these horses under cover."

He held out his hand for each of us to shake, his warm blue eyes smiling into mine when my turn came, and despite myself, I felt charmed. I was beginning to agree with everybody else: Will George couldn't have done it.

Lonny and I hurried to get into the pickup as rain spattered the windshield; my last sight of Will George was a cowboy-hatted figure on a galloping sorrel mare, waving his help inside the barn. He looked more like a hero than a villain.

THIRTEEN

An hour later rain was pouring down all around us, rattling on the roof of the truck, and the asphalt road was wet and black, the sky opaquely gray. Water sluiced down the windshield and the wipers squeegeed back and forth. Lonny and I sipped hot coffee out of paper cups, Blue curled comfortably on the seat between us, his chin on Lonny's thigh. I drove slowly, straining a little to see through the storm.

We were rolling down the western slope of Pacheco Pass, headed back to the coast, after eating lunch at the Woolgrower's, a Basque restaurant that offered a single multicourse meal served at long tables with red-and-white checked cloths and featuring every type of red meat known to man (delicious, even if currently unfashionable). I felt contentedly full, and ready to investigate a little more.

"Can you handle posing as a cutting horse buyer?" I asked Lonny. "Or the boyfriend of one?"

"Depends." He smiled.

"It won't take long. I want to swing by Salinas, talk to Jay Holley. He's the guy Bret used to work for."

"Why?"

"I don't know. Beat the bushes, see what flies out. Bret called Jay 'Will's protégé,' and said that Casey called Jay the night before he was killed."

"Don't tell me. You want to add Jay Holley to your suspect list."

"I don't have any better ideas, at this point. The colt in Will's barn was a three-year-old, that's for sure. Maybe all this ringer talk is so much bullshit. Maybe Melissa's right, and Casey did have a bee in his bonnet about Will George. But Casey's dead."

"That's the point," Lonny said slowly. "He's dead—after flinging all these accusations around."

Silence followed that remark. Lonny rubbed Blue's head; Blue was pressing his chin against Lonny's knee, his ears folded back in a supplicating pose that invited rubbing. Clearly Lonny had made Blue's approved list.

"So let's go see Jay Holley." Lonny's eyes crinkled at the corners. "It's on the way home, anyway, more or less."

Salinas was actually an hour south of Santa Cruz, a city that was Watsonville's spiritual sister; it dominated the agricultural Salinas Valley as Watsonville did the Pajaro Valley. Santa Cruz and Monterey sat up at the north and south points of the bay respectively, looking out on the water—pretty, picturesque, the destinations of tourists—and inland, between them, were Watsonville and Salinas—plain and unpretentious centers for farming and industry. Salinas, in particular, fancied itself a cowboy town, was home to the Salinas Rodeo, and boasted a good many more cowhorse trainers than Watsonville, where Casey Brooks had been something of an iconoclast.

Salinas was not exactly on the route back to Santa Cruz, but we didn't have to detour more than an hour out of our way to drop by the Salinas River Ranch, where Jay Holley trained cutting horses. Bret had given me directions this morning, and I had no trouble finding the place, despite driving winding, wet back roads along the sandy Salinas River for several miles before we saw the old-fashioned ranch entrance—two tall wooden posts with a cross member high above from which hung a now-illegible painted wooden sign.

"This is it," I said as we turned in.

Lonny looked out the window curiously as we bumped down a badly maintained dirt road, already turning greasy in the rain despite a minimal coating of gravel, and pulled into an old-fashioned-looking barnyard with a peeling white two-story Victorian-type house, two huge old wooden barns with tin roofs, and a wide assortment of corrals, arenas, sheds and pens—all apparently built at different times and of different materials.

"Not quite in Will's league, is he?" I said as we peered through the slanting gray rain at the Salinas River Ranch.

Lonny shook his head no.

The barnyard appeared deserted; no human beings in sight. A black-and-white ranch dog, the usual border collie cross, barked apathetically at us for a minute—Blue's ears pricked up and he growled softly at the sound—then scurried back into the bigger of the two barns, out of the rain. As I watched, a figure stepped into the open doorway of the barn and looked to see who'd pulled into his yard. It appeared to be the man I'd seen at the cutting.

He came walking out toward the truck, calling to the dog to hush up and peering curiously at the rainy windshield. I got out, Lonny following suit, and, holding my slicker over my head, moved in his direction. He motioned us toward the open barn door and we hurried after him.

Once inside, I shook water droplets off my hair and looked at the man in front of me. Pale skin, pale hair, water dripping from the brim of his gray cowboy hat, those oddly cold blue eyes contrasting with the grinning, thin-lipped mouth—it was Jay Holley.

"Hi," I said. "I'm Gail McCarthy. I'm interested in buying a cutting horse, and Bret Boncantini said I should see you."

The grin got wider. He tipped his hat slightly and said, "Nice to meet you, ma'am. I'm Jay Holley."

Lonny held out his hand. "Lonny Peterson."

The two men shook. I noticed Jay hadn't offered to shake my hand, but then, I hadn't offered, either.

Jay launched into a salesman's spiel before I could begin to say anything more, for which I was profoundly grateful, as I wasn't sure exactly what to say. His face was animated as he talked, and he smiled a lot; Jay Holley, unlike Will George, seemed extremely enthusiastic about selling me a horse. Judging by his surroundings, he might have welcomed an infusion of cash.

Sagging above us, the roof of the tackroom where we stood was already leaking in several places—steady drips that were plopping into various pots and pans. Through an open archway I could see into the big, dim interior of the old barn, an enormous dusky cavern with a motley collection of pens that looked baling-wired together crowding the space—a horse in every pen, I noticed. The view out the door was of rain still pouring down; an outdoor arena that could pass for a holding pond about now appeared less than useful for winter training. I couldn't see a covered arena anywhere.

I tuned back in to hear Jay Holley saying, "So both these mares could fit you; they'd both be good for a beginner. I'd saddle them up and let you try them right now, but . . ." He waved a dismissive hand at the weather.

Trying for a casual tone, I said, "I'll come back another time, maybe. I was going to stop on my way home and see someone named Casey Brooks; Bret said he was a cowhorse trainer, too. Do you know him?"

Emotions rippled across Jay Holley's face. It was a shut-in face, a face that, under its superficial good humor, looked clenched and defensive—those icy eyes gave the game away; they never smiled when the mouth did. My words had startled him, though. Consternation, dismay, and indecision showed clearly, and for a second Jay Holley looked the twenty-five or so he probably was, rather than a prematurely aged and hardened thirty-five.

"Casey Brooks is dead." He said it matter-of-factly. After a moment: "A horse killed him; that's what I heard."

I pretended the conventional shock I thought appropriate and tried not to meet Lonny's eyes. "How grim. Is that common?"

Jay Holley's mouth twitched in a pitying way at my ignorance. "No, ma'am, it's not. I heard he was killed in a fall off a broke horse. Bret told me, as a matter of fact." He looked curiously at me. "Bret's a friend of yours?"

"Yep. Old friend."

Jay Holley looked as if he wondered what kind of friend, but went on after a minute. "I was real surprised to hear about Casey, to tell the truth. He called me the night before, the night before he was killed, I guess."

"Oh. What about?" And why in the world would it be any business of mine, I thought, but Jay didn't seem to think the question inappropriately nosy.

"Wanted to know what I knew about a horse. A horse that won the West Coast Futurity for Will George."

"How interesting. I just went by to see Will George. Looking at horses." I added, "He showed me the horse he won on."

Jay nodded. "Casey wanted to know if I'd ridden that horse for Will, which I hadn't. Wanted to know all about him. Said he had had him when he was a two-year-old and was interested in him. I couldn't tell him much. I was at the futurity and saw the horse work, and I know Will was surprised the colt did as well as he did. Will told me that he didn't know the horse very well; somebody had been riding it for him, I think, but he didn't mention who. He said he didn't think much of its chances—guess it surprised him." Jay laughed.

"Bret told me," I said carefully, "that Casey thought that horse was pretty good as a two-year-old."

"Yeah, that's what he said." Jay shrugged. "Horses change, and everybody likes something different. Maybe the horse wasn't Will's type of horse. Looks like Casey was right about him, though." He shrugged again, then shifted gears and became animated. "Like that first mare I was telling you about. The girl that had her didn't get along with her at all, but I think she'd really be a good horse for the right person. I placed on her last weekend in the novice class, and . . ."

Tuning him out again as he launched off into another enthusiastic sales pitch, I listened for more polite minutes and, after a tour of the barn and an inspection of the two mares he wanted to sell me, made my excuses and left, Lonny in tow.

Back in the truck, slithering down the wet road with Blue standing half on my lap, craning for another view of the ranch dog, I cast a glance at Lonny's quiet profile.

"Well, that didn't accomplish much." I knew I sounded peeved.

Lonny grinned at me. "You mean you didn't see any cutting horses you'd like?"

"You know what I mean. And I wouldn't mind a cutting horse, thank you. But I can't afford one; I can barely afford the horse I've got. I was just trying to pitch a rock into a yellow jacket's nest and see what flew out. Only nothing happened."

Lonny sighed. "I still don't think much of your idea that Casey was murdered, but if you're determined to suspect someone, why don't you work on the girlfriend—if you go by the book, she's the likeliest candidate."

"All right, I'll concentrate on Melissa. Where do I start?"

"Motive, opportunity, ability to commit the crime, evidence linking her to the scene of the crime . . . how's that?"

"Motive," I started, ticking them off on my fingers. "Well, she had about as much motive as anybody does who's in a relationship that's not working out. I guess you could call that a motive. Opportunity, yeah, I guess so. She wasn't around that morning when I found Casey, and she knew he was going to ride Shiloh and what route he usually took . . . Hey, that's a good point," I said, suddenly struck. "Not everybody would have known where to wait for him along that trail. I'm not sure Will George would. But Melissa would have known for sure."

"All right. Could she have killed him?"

"Almost anybody could have. Melissa's more than fit enough to throw a rock. It's hard to picture her doing it, though. And there's another thing. Melissa would never have poisoned those horses. She might have cut the cinch, but poison horses—not a chance."

"Why's that?"

"She just wouldn't, that's all. She was the one who was really upset when I had to put the one horse down—much more than Casey. She loves horses, loves the horse business. I can see her killing Casey, but no way would she have poisoned those horses."

"That's a moral system for you. But let's say she didn't poison the horses. She could still have murdered Casey. The horses could have been poisoned by someone else."

"I don't think so. Call it instinct. I think the same person did both."

"Or someone poisoned the horses and Casey died by accident."

I shook my head dubiously. "I guess all I have to go on is my same old instinct, but it just seems wrong to me."

Fortunately for the future of our relationship, Lonny didn't say anything derogatory about women's intuition. "Then you need a suspect who has a motive both for poisoning the horses and for killing Casey."

"I've got one," I said slowly.

Lonny looked inquiringly in my direction. "Who are we talking about now?"

"Martha Welch."

"Mrs. Gotrocks?"

I glanced at him curiously. "That's what Bret called her."

Lonny's face creased into a wide grin. "I'm amazed you don't know her. I thought everybody in the horse business in Santa Cruz County knew old Martha."

"Why should I?"

"She's legendary. She's been through several husbands, dozens of horse trainers, at least a half dozen vets. That's probably why you don't know her; I think she quit Jim several years ago. She can't get along with anybody. But what gives her a motive to kill Casey Brooks?"

"One of the horses that died belonged to her. Melissa said the horse was insured for a lot—more than it was worth. If Martha Welch wanted to kill it for the insurance money, it makes sense that she'd kill a bunch of the others so it didn't look like hers was a particular target. Of course, if she's as rich as everyone says, she wouldn't need the insurance money."

"Oh, I don't know about that. Martha's as notorious for being tight as she is for being rich. Most of her long string of disagreements were over money."

"She made out that she was angry at Casey about her horse dying," I went on, "but that could have been an act.

She *was* upset with Casey, though. It was written all over her. She'd probably know what trail he usually took if she had a horse in training with him. Maybe he threatened to turn her in."

I glanced at Lonny speculatively. "Do you know where she lives?"

"Sure." Lonny had no trouble interpreting my look. "But what excuse do you have for going there? She doesn't use Jim as her vet anymore."

"No problem. I'm the vet that put her horse down, remember? I can say the insurance people called me. You know, it's kind of funny they haven't. Ken Resavich's insurance company contacted me right away about his horses."

Lonny sighed and scratched Blue's ears. "All right. I'll direct you to Martha's. But this is it. This is absolutely the last person we try and pin a murder on. Agreed?"

"It's a deal."

FOURTEEN

Martha Welch turned out to live in south Santa Cruz County, high in the hills behind Watsonville, not all that far from Ken Resavich. That argued well for my suspicions.

I drove the winding, narrow curves of Mt. Madonna Road at a crawl; the rain was still drumming down and visibility was terrible. Lonny directed me to an innocuous wooden gate between two redwood trees. The gate was standing open and a slender paved drive, slick with rain, led off between ranks of other redwoods, somber dark pillars in the gray.

"This doesn't look like a wealthy person's place," I commented, as I nosed the truck down the drive.

"You'll see." Lonny's voice was amused.

The road twisted between redwood groves; the woods around us peaceful and pristine in the rain—undisturbed wilderness, no house or garden or cultivation in sight. We'd gone at least half a mile before a rail fence appeared on our right, then our left, lining the road. The boards were natural, unpainted wood, like the gate, and blended easily into the surroundings. Inside the fences were wide pastures, and in the pastures were horses. Broodmares, weanlings and yearlings, I judged, arrayed in different fields according to type and looking wet but not unhappy in the streaming rain. Horses, I'd noticed, didn't mind being out in the rain, unless it was accompanied by extreme cold or high winds.

Another half mile or so between the pastures, then the drive rose out of a little dip; I almost skidded to a halt.

"Holy cow," I breathed.

"See what I mean." Lonny was enjoying my reaction.

One came upon Martha Welch's place suddenly—from the crest of the little dip, her house and barnyard were laid out in front and below the approaching vehicle in all their simple splendor. This was a far cry from Will George's kind of money. His place had been ostentatiously wealthy, advertising his success, nouveau riche if ever I had seen it. Martha Welch's was just the opposite.

A large, one-story, rambling house was situated on the slight slope, and the arms and branches of the building followed the little ridges and descents of the land, so that the house was constantly moving up and down a step or two. Shingled all over, the shingles stained a natural wood color like the fences, the house had no less than six gray stone chimneys, no more than ten doors. All the windows, of which there were many, had a latticework of small panes, the framework painted white—the whole place looked vaguely like a hunting lodge that Louis XIV would have used.

Small lawns and flowering plantings nestled in the bays between the various wings of the building, and across an acre or so of paved courtyard sat a pretty two-story barn, also shingled, with what was obviously living quarters up above it. Wide decks ran around the house on the far side, extending into a space that overlooked the whole panorama of the Monterey Bay.

It was the bay that lent this house its breathtaking drama;

the house itself was carefully and expensively understated, its focal point a vista of hills tumbling down to the sweep of the coastline. From the house one could see everything—the half moon of the bay, Santa Cruz to the north and Monterey to the south—rendered even more dramatic this afternoon by the storm clouds scudding across the sky.

For a few minutes, I simply sat and stared.

"Pretty, isn't it?" Lonny's voice was amused.

"I guess. It's beautiful."

"Her parents built it. Her dad was a grandson of one of the original logging barons of the West Coast. Martha is his only child."

"Wow." I stepped gently on the accelerator and drove up to the house, trying not to feel intimidated. Martha Welch could be arrested for murder just like anybody else, I reminded myself.

One of the big, dark gray clouds seemed to break in two right over us, and a deluge was pouring down as I parked the truck in front of the house. Pulling my slicker on as I got out, I was about to dash for the front door when a figure came flying out of the barn, yelling in our direction.

"You're a vet, aren't you?" The shouted question was addressed to Lonny, not me. "Come quick!"

Startled, I peered through the rain at a woman I recognized as Martha Welch. Realizing that she'd identified the multicompartmented cover on my pickup bed as that of a veterinarian, I nodded affirmatively. "I'm a vet. What's the matter?"

She wasn't listening. "Quick, come out here. She'll bleed to death!"

Martha dashed back through the rain toward her barn; I grabbed some tranquilizers and suturing equipment and followed at the run, Lonny beside me.

"She" proved to be a dun mare with a deep cut on her right front pastern, a cut that was squirting a veritable red fountain of blood with every beat of her heart. Artery, I thought.

Stepping up to the mare, who was tossing her head and dancing frantically in circles, spraying blood in all directions, I told a very young man with a cowboy hat who had the look of an aspiring trainer and was holding the lead rope, "Keep her as still as you can so I can get this injection in her jugular vein."

Martha Welch gave me a sharp look. "Are you the vet?" Her eyes moved questioningly to Lonny.

"Yes, I am."

"Well, get on with it then. Quick. Before she bleeds to death."

It would be a while before she'd bleed to death, I thought, but I kept my mouth shut. Steadying the mare's head a little, I inserted the needle in the underside of her neck with a quick plink, attached the syringe and withdrew enough blood to be sure I'd hit the jugular vein, then injected rompin, a tranquilizer that rendered frantic horses relaxed and immobile. In a minute the mare was swaying on her feet, head down, oblivious to her cut leg and everything else.

I knelt beside her and clamped off the squirting artery, eliminating the bloody fountain. Using clean gauze pads to mop up most of the mess, I began suturing the wound together. Once sutured, I wrapped it with a bandage to protect it, Lonny bringing me the necessary materials from my truck. Martha Welch watched the whole operation with a silent but critical eye.

When I was done, I stood up and smiled at her. "I'm Gail McCarthy, and this is Lonny Peterson."

"Martha Welch. Thank you. That's one of my best broodmares. She was tied here in the barn; this idiot left a hoe where she could step on it." She gestured in a derogatory way at the young man in the cowboy hat, who winced and quickly led the mare away.

Now that her face was no longer distorted by distress, Martha Welch appeared a firmly elegant woman of indeterminate middle age, though the elegance was not a type I admired. Gold and diamonds sparkled from her ears, hung about her neck, and encrusted her fingers—it was evident where the nickname "Mrs. Gotrocks" had come from. Her hair looked crisp and unmessable despite her run through the rain, and her face was stretched tight and masked with make-up—one of the reasons her age was in question. A fit-looking figure said aerobics and maybe a few tucks. Martha Welch was anywhere between forty-five and sixty-five, and obviously determined not to get any older.

"I work for Jim Leonard," I went on conversationally, using a handful of gauze to wipe some blood off my boots.

"I suppose Jim will be sending me a bill." Martha Welch sounded disgruntled, and I noticed Lonny was having a hard time hiding his smile.

"Not necessarily," I said, thinking fast. "I came up here to ask you about another matter. Perhaps," I laid careful stress on the *perhaps,* "I could just do this as a favor. I'm not officially at work today."

The idea of what was undoubtedly a hundred-dollar-plus veterinary bill being written off like that roused Martha Welch to quick hospitality. "Why don't you come inside," she indicated both Lonny and me with a wave of her arm, "where we can be more comfortable."

Rain was still spitting fitfully as we crossed the courtyard; large, purplish clouds hanging over the bay seemed to indicate that more storm was on its way. Leaving my blood-spattered slicker in the pickup, I followed Lonny through the front door of Martha Welch's house, wiping my feet carefully on the doormat, and stopping to wash my hands in a sparkling little guest bathroom.

We were led into a room at the end of an arm of the house that stretched out toward the bay—a wonderful room, a room I'd have given my eye teeth for. Smallish, but high-ceilinged—I supposed you could call it a sitting room; a couch, two or three armchairs, and a stone fireplace (with a pleasant fire flickering in it) filled the available space. The floors were wide-planked oak, polished to a soft sheen, the walls and ceiling natural wood, the open-beam rafters shadowy above us. All the furniture was covered with a bright floral print—rust red on deep green—that was just colorful enough to be cheerful and pleasing rather than garish against the simple wood-toned walls. Martha Welch switched on a lamp on a small table and gestured at the furniture. I sat down in an armchair and stared.

Across the front of this room was a wall of windows, delicately lattice-paned; beyond the windows the Monterey Bay stretched in its full glory, with the coastal hills and the Pajaro Valley in the foreground. The first storm of the season rambled across an immensity of sky and space and I felt a sense of delight. If I owned this house, I thought, I'd sit in this room every evening with a glass of wine and watch the light die out of the west.

It appeared that I was going to get to do this at least once, as Martha Welch was offering us a drink. "Chardonnay, if you have it," I requested.

A yell of "Nancy," followed by our drink orders, informed me that she probably did have it.

Lonny had seated himself in an armchair; Martha Welch chose the couch and settled herself in one corner, crossing a leg with a self-conscious attempt at casualness.

As an effort at relaxation, it was largely a failure; the tension in the woman was obvious. I more or less suspected that it was habitual; Martha Welch had the appearance of someone who would never truly relax, even drinking a solitary cup of coffee, or sitting alone in the evening, she would be filled with nervous energy.

A fiftyish woman brought our drinks on a tray; I sipped

my wine, Lonny had a bourbon and soda, Martha Welch had called for an old-fashioned. It all felt very civilized. I wasn't sure how to begin.

"I'm the vet that Casey Brooks used," was what I tried, and it elicited all the reaction that my interviews with Will George and Jay Holley had failed to provoke.

Martha Welch stiffened in her corner; her lips tightened and her eyes flashed. "What did he do, tell you I poisoned my own horse?"

I was taken aback. "Well, no."

"He had the nerve to say that to me, the bastard."

"Casey's dead, you know." I watched curiously for her reaction.

She had the grace to look slightly abashed. "I heard." I had the impression she would have liked to say "good riddance to bad rubbish," but she didn't. She said, "Did he tell you not to sign the certificate for the insurance?" Before I could decide what answer to make, she went on. "Because I'm not putting up with that. Dead or not, Casey Brooks is not causing me any more trouble."

Martha Welch looked hostile, defiant and unrepentant—her emotions all in full view. She'd as good as admitted a motive for murdering Casey, and it didn't seem to bother her at all. There was something odd in what she'd said, though.

"It was my impression Casey thought Will George poisoned those horses," I said carefully.

Martha Welch snorted. "It's a rough thing to say about somebody who's dead, but Casey was a damn fool. He *was* going around telling everyone that Will George did it, which is obviously ridiculous, and when he couldn't make enough trouble that way, he accused me of poisoning my own horse."

I stared at her. Somehow that didn't go with the Casey I

had known. Hardheaded, egotistical, abrasive, yes—but making trouble just for the sake of it, no.

She was still talking. "Will George would never have poisoned those horses, any more than I would. I called him and told him what Casey was saying about him. He just laughed."

That was interesting. Will George had known that Casey suspected him—Will George who had turned his quiet, blue-eyed gaze on me and said only, "He was a good hand," of Casey. Will George was not a man who would rattle easily.

Martha Welch, on the other hand, seemed quite "rattleable." I tried to picture her poisoning the horses, cutting the cinch, braining Casey with a rock. It was possible. There was a sense of suppressed violence in this woman, only half hidden under her polished exterior. She was strung tight as a piano wire; if the wire snapped, what sort of fury would be unleashed?

"You *are* planning on signing the insurance forms, aren't you?" She was fixing me with a steely eye.

Lonny smiled at me behind his drink; he'd very carefully kept out of this conversation, I'd noticed, as he had the last one. All this amateur detective work probably wasn't something he wanted to be involved with. He looked amused, though.

"The horse was poisoned," I told Martha Welch frankly. "But I have no reason to believe you had anything to do with it."

"You're damn right I didn't. I don't believe it was poisoned, anyway. All I'm interested in is that you sign the paperwork stating it needed to be destroyed."

I considered arguing the point that poisoning was indisputable given the test results, and gave it up as a bad idea. She wouldn't listen.

"The horse did need to be put down, I'll agree to that," I said calmly.

"I'll have the company send you the paperwork right away." She took a final swallow of her drink and stood up. Clearly, as far as she was concerned, the interview was at an end.

Draining the last of my chardonnay and taking a regretful glance at the view, I followed her to the door, Lonny accompanying me silently. When we were back in the truck he looked over at me. "What do you think?" I could hear the humor in his voice.

"Beats me. She's got a motive, all right. I can't check her for an alibi, which would be the next step; I'm not a cop. I need to interest that detective in finding out where some of these people were when Casey was killed. That would help."

"Good luck."

"Thanks a lot. I can tell you don't think she'll be interested." I looked at Lonny curiously. "Don't you care? Don't you want Casey's murderer, if there was a murderer, to be caught?"

"Care? Sure, I care. But unlike you, I don't think he was murdered. And if he was, I still say, I'll pick the girlfriend every time."

FIFTEEN

Renewed gusts of rain spattered the windshield as I drove slowly down the loops and twists of Mt. Madonna Road. Evening was closing in and the sky was a dark and unrelieved gray. I felt a sense of depression. All my detective work hadn't come to much. I was hungry and tired of driving and I wanted to be cheered up.

As if he'd read my thoughts, Lonny asked, "How about a home-cooked meal?"

"Sounds great."

"Spaghetti and red wine—real stormy night food. In front of the fire. I make a mean spaghetti."

I smiled at him gratefully. "You're on."

Lonny's house welcomed us when I pulled up in front of it; he'd left a couple of lamps on and the curtains open, and the cozy front room appeared a safe haven in the blowing rain.

I got out of the truck feeling stiff and sore, and Blue slid out after me, stiffer than I was. He hobbled around in the rain peeing on my tires, then wagged his stump of a tail to indicate he wanted back in the cab.

"Long day, huh, boy," I told him, scratching him behind the ears.

He licked my hand and curled up on the seat of the truck with a grunt, apparently prepared to nap a few more hours. There were some advantages to being an old dog, I thought, as I cracked the windows a hair. Patience being one of them.

Walking through the front door of Lonny's house I was greeted with a meow by the big pinkish beige cat who had jumped on his lap the other night. Sam, I remembered. Following the cat was a creature no larger than my hand, the color and texture of an animated dust ball. It mewed, giving me a clue to its identity.

"What's that?" I laughed.

"That's a cat," Lonny said with a proprietary grin. "What do you mean 'What's that?' That's Gandalf."

The little creature was mewing and rubbing itself on Lonny's legs in a miniature imitation of Sam, who seemed to regard it with tolerant disdain. Lonny petted both cats and picked up the little one. "I found him two nights ago. I was at the barn feeding the horses their dinner; it was black dark, no moon at all, and I heard this meowing. I couldn't see a thing, but I tracked him down by all the noise he was making. He was just marching along the road screeching his head off. I scooped him up and brought him home."

"Lucky for him." I petted the little cat, who purred at me from his seat in Lonny's palm; his eyes squinted shut in a cat smile of happiness.

"Sit down by the woodstove, if you like," Lonny told me, taking in, I suppose, my weary expression. "I'll bring you a glass of wine and build us a fire."

"Thanks." I settled myself on the couch, accepted a glass of chianti, and watched him lay split kindling and strike a match. The primitive ritual was deeply comforting; small flames flickered and grew until the wood was crackling happily and orangey fire shadows danced on the walls. Safety and warmth in the threatening night. I sipped the almost bitter red wine and listened to the rain on the roof and felt a growing sense of contentment.

Lonny started making spaghetti in the kitchen and the simmering sweet smell of onions in olive oil crept into the living room. During a break in the storm I fed Lonny's horses, then sat and watched the fire some more, sipping a second glass of chianti and talking to Lonny as he made dinner, which proved to be terrific. His spaghetti was like a stew, thick with spicy Italian sausage, bell pepper, onion and mushrooms. When we were done I brought Blue into the house on his leash, feeling that he'd spent enough of the day cooped up in the truck, but unwilling to trust the cats to his mercies. Blue liked cats just fine; he especially liked them when they were running away from him.

Lonny and I sat in companionable silence by the fire for a while, watching Gandalf play with Blue. Confined by his leash, the old dog was no danger; he snapped gently at the kitten, who didn't seem in the least afraid of him. The tiny gray paws batted at Blue's old speckled muzzle, and the two animals seemed content to play predator/prey games together, with no intent or fear of harm.

"Do you want to stay?" Lonny was nothing if not direct.

"I don't know." I felt deeply peaceful and realized I did want to stay; at least, I didn't want to leave. It struck me that the time had passed for saying no to Lonny, if I wanted to keep growing closer to him rather than start pulling away. But I was still scared of the consequences of that closeness.

"I do want to stay," I told him honestly. "I'm just afraid to."

His face was turned toward me, his eyes serious. After a minute he said, "Stay with me. Just hold me, that's all."

Feeling confused, I asked, "What do you mean?"

"What I said. Sleep in my bed. Hold me. The rest of it will keep."

"I thought the rest of it was the main point."

"When you're ready. I want to be close to you, Gail, I want to love you. But I want it when it's right. Tonight let's just sleep together."

"All right," I told him, taking his hand. "If you think we can."

"We can." He grinned. "Once."

Which was how I came to spend the night in Lonny's bed, pressed up against the warmth of his body, while the rain pattered on the roof and the light from the fire flickered through the open door. Somehow—I never really understood how—sex was present but kept comfortably at bay, and a sense of peaceful connectedness grew in me until I relaxed and fell asleep, happier than I could remember being.

I woke up the next morning with my back pressed against Lonny's stomach, spoon fashion, and his arms wrapped around me. This might have led to more interesting things except it was four-thirty in the morning and the alarm which had woken me was shrilling insistently.

Lonny gave me a final affectionate rub and got out of bed. "I'm leaving this morning for the mountains, did I tell you?"

"Not that I remember," I mumbled sleepily. "Did you say why?"

"Oh, business." Lonny was pulling his jeans on and didn't look at me; I sensed evasiveness.

"Just what is your business?" I smiled up at him, trying to take the nosy sting out of my question. "I'm starting to be afraid you're a hit man for the mob."

"Nothing so glamorous." Lonny sat down heavily on the edge of the bed and looked at me.

No doubt I looked rumpled, I thought distractedly, but there wasn't much I could do about it. "You said you used to be a packer; that's all you've ever mentioned, and you're obviously not a packer now."

"Well I am, actually. I own a pack station. Crazy Horse Creek. I don't run it anymore; I've got a partner who does that. I go up every month or so to check in with him, make sure things are going all right. I'll be gone for most of this week." There was a tone in Lonny's voice that was hard to place. Hesitant. Tentative.

"You own a pack station? That sounds interesting," I prodded.

Lonny seemed to be watching me closely; the expression in his eyes was vulnerable. "It is interesting to me. It broke up my marriage, though. My wife did not want to be married to a packer, and she didn't want to live in a rundown old resort in the mountains. What she wanted was a life on the coast with a man who had a respectable profession. It's one of the reasons I retired. Didn't help, though." He laughed briefly. "She left me to live with a doctor."

"Is that the reason you didn't want to tell me what you did for a living?" I asked curiously.

"Sure. You're a vet; you've got eight years' worth of college education, you're a doctor in your own right. I quit high school when I was sixteen and made my money packing horses."

I chose my words carefully. "That doesn't matter, as far as I'm concerned. And I'd say you made pretty good money packing horses."

Lonny smiled. "I did at that. Crazy Horse Creek is the biggest pack station in the Sierras now; it's making a good living for both my partner and me. It wasn't always that way. When I was in my twenties, I worked round the clock, and we didn't have a nickel to spare. It was hard on Sara."

Sara, I thought. Her name is Sara. Suddenly I felt uncomfortable, as though I were lying in Sara's bed.

Lonny smiled down at me. "What are you going to do today? Keep on playing detective?"

"Oh, I don't know," I grimaced up at him from the bed. "There's so much I need to find out; trying to look into this is beginning to seem pretty pointless."

Lonny leaned down and kissed me. "I can think of better things for you to do."

"I'm sure you can. I can think of better things for me to do, too. Like concentrate on my job. Which, little though it pays, pays a whole lot better than amateur detective work. It's just that Casey . . ." I stopped, unable to finish the sentence. That Casey hadn't wanted to die, my mind said. That I was angry at all that talent snuffed out, that Casey wasn't meant to be dead. If someone had killed him, I would find out who.

Getting out of bed, I enjoyed Lonny's admiring glance at my partially clothed body as I pulled my sweater on. I put my arms around him briefly and kissed him. "Thank you," I said, "that was nice."

He knew what I meant. "Trial run. I'll give you a call when I get back?"

"Right."

The smile between us then was intimate, shared, a result of that connectedness I'd felt last night, and I thought that Sara or no Sara, everything had changed. For the better.

SIXTEEN

I walked in my own front door at eight o'clock that sunny rain-washed morning; Lonny and I had shared coffee and rolls at a local bakery before he took off for the mountains, and I felt warm and sated. Belting out "Red River Valley" as I started doing the dishes, I was grateful for Bret's conspicuous absence. I can't carry a tune, but I like to sing—when I'm alone.

Judging by the sleeping bag and piles of clothes scattered around the living room, I wasn't done with my boarder yet. He'd probably found a new girl, but in all likelihood it would be a one-night relationship.

Ah well, none of my business. Except I didn't want him living here forever. I shuffled his stuff into one pile and cleaned the living room, thinking of Lonny. Would I want Lonny living here forever? I didn't know, but I enjoyed considering the question.

When the house was neat, I gave serious thought to the day. Detective work? Staring at my pager, which sat on the kitchen table, black and implacable, I realized I'd have to stick to in-county investigating. Jim and I took it in turn to be on call on Sundays, and today was my turn. Sure as hell that pager would beep if I left the general vicinity of Santa Cruz.

As it happened, I wasn't given a lot of time to worry about it. I'd barely finished making my grocery list when the pager shrilled in its determined, insistent way—that sound so familiar to overworked veterinarians.

The caller turned out to be a woman whose gelding had a swollen sheath, one of those nonemergency "emergencies" we got from time to time. I explained patiently and at length that a swollen sheath was not, generally speaking, a problem which needed immediate attention; the horse's sheath would have to get as big or bigger than a cantaloupe for there to be any question of him having a problem urinating.

To no avail. The woman wasn't listening. She talked over me and through me, repeating that she was worried about her poor horse and thought he must be miserable.

After telling her that it would cost her sixty extra dollars just to have me set foot on her place for an emergency call, I agreed that I would certainly come see her horse if she wanted me to, and got in my truck, cursing at the stupidity of people in general.

The rest of the day turned out to be like that. I washed the gelding's sheath—a process which the woman could easily have done herself—reassured her that he would be fine, and before I could get back in my truck the pager beeped again. This time it was a client with a horse who had been lame for a week, but today he was "suddenly worse."

I asked questions; the information I elicited was vague, but this horse didn't sound like a true emergency either. Once again I explained about the extra costs of an emergency call; a very common scenario involved a client who'd demanded the vet come out for an "emergency" refusing to pay the bill on the grounds that the charges were too high for what little minor work the veterinarian had actually had to do. But once again, the woman on the phone was sure that I should come out right away.

I drove the hour and a half that it took me to get from Watsonville, where the horse with the swollen sheath was, to Boulder Creek, high in the mountains of the north county, thinking while I did it that this was probably going to prove to be another waste of time and money. This call was actually even worse, as the horse turned out to be only slightly lame, and I was unable to determine what was wrong with him without x-rays, which the woman refused to have, saying they "cost too much."

Not bothering to question the logic of spending sixty unnecessary dollars to get me out here on a Sunday but being unwilling to spend a hundred dollars to get some information that might actually help to diagnose her horse, I took my leave as gracefully as I could, telling her to call me if she changed her mind. Sure enough, the pager buzzed when I was halfway back to Santa Cruz.

Back I went; then out to two more calls, only one of which was a true emergency. This horse, a Peruvian Paso, had a sand colic that looked bad. I treated him as well as I could and told the people that if he got worse they would have to send him to the veterinary emergency center at Davis for a possible operation. This they obdurately refused to consider—again, too much money—and I drove out past the elaborate garden and what looked like a mansion gnashing my teeth. Some days were just like this.

It was almost five o'clock and I hadn't had much lunch—just a bag of chips and a mineral water, grabbed on the way to somewhere. Pushing the depressing memories of my day away from me, I stopped at Carpo's for dinner.

Carpo's is an institution in Soquel. A remodeled burger joint, it offers Santa Cruz–style fast food at prices even an underpaid vet can afford. Waiting through the usual long line, I virtuously ordered a salad bar to go with my glass of chardonnay—not such a hardship at Carpo's, as the salad bar was varied and featured terrific whole wheat sourdough bread.

Carrying my assembled salad around the restaurant, looking for the always-hard-to-find empty table, I spotted a familiar face. Snub nose, wavy well-cut blonde hair—it was Detective Ward.

She was sitting alone at a table near a window, reading the paper. There was a glass of red wine in front of her, and as I watched, she reached a hand out to take a sip without looking up. She seemed absorbed and content, and I hesitated, wondering whether to disturb her in her private time. On the other hand, the sight of her brought what seemed like dozens of questions and ideas tumbling into my mind, questions that had disappeared in the hubbub of the day, but were still hanging there, unanswered.

Detective Ward looked up suddenly and our eyes met. For a second hers were puzzled, but then I saw what I was sure was a flash of recognition before her face became expressionless.

I nodded at her civilly. "Detective Ward. I'm Doctor McCarthy. Do you mind if I sit with you?"

She glanced around the restaurant, which was demonstrably crowded, and then back at me. "Of course not."

I sat down and we studied each other for a moment with what I thought was equal curiosity on both parts. She was as well dressed as when I had first seen her—medium gray lightweight wool suit, pale gray man-tailored shirt, a heavy braided gold chain around her neck that picked up the gold highlights in her hair. Career clothes. Apparently she worked Sundays, too.

Wondering what she would make of my definitely *not* dressed-for-success appearance, I had the impulse to wish that the last call of the day hadn't included an enthusiastic

Labrador who'd jumped up on me and spattered my jeans with mud. I knew I looked casual, crumpled, and not too clean, but there was nothing I could do about it at the moment.

The silent inventory had gone on long enough. I smiled at her and said, "I'm glad I saw you here. I was planning to go down to the sheriff's office and just got too busy." The part about the sheriff's office was an outright lie, but what the hell. I certainly had been busy.

She raised noncommittal eyes to my face. "Oh?"

I took a sip of wine. "I've found out some things that I think you should know, if you don't already."

She studied me with the expression of a woman being bothered by a pesky mosquito, uncertain whether to swat or ignore, but obviously exasperated.

"What things are these?" was what she said.

I told her everything I knew about Casey Brooks, between sips of wine and mouthfuls of salad and bread. Ignoring her pained expression, I waded through his accusations of Will George, his stormy relationship with Melissa, and his quarrel with Martha Welch. Allowing Detective Ward to escape only long enough to pick up her calamari and pasta when it was ready, I elaborated on the poisoned horses, the cut cinch, the unlikeliness of Shiloh ever dislodging Casey, talked at length about the hiding places along the trail and the wide choice of projectiles, went quickly through my interviews with Will George, Jay Holley, and Martha Welch. Finishing up my summary, I told my less-than-riveted audience, "That's about all I know. It seems suspicious to me, but, as you can tell, I don't have any proof, and there are a lot of things I need to know and don't. Like whether any or all of the suspects have alibis. And who may have had something to gain from Casey's death that I don't know about. Who inherited his money, if he had any. Does he have any family? I don't even know that."

In the course of my conversation—monologue, really—Detective Ward's expression had shifted from pained to resigned; now she forked up the last of her calamari and gave me a look that was both quizzical and irritated.

"So you feel the sheriff's department should do some legwork for you, is that it?" Her voice was cool.

I swallowed my remaining wine and fought to keep my temper. "Not exactly. I wanted to give you what information I had. Maybe—I'm not saying you have any obligation—you would be comfortable giving me the answers to some of those questions, supposing you knew them."

Detective Ward looked at me and sighed. Without saying anything she pushed her plate aside and reached for her purse, and I had the sense she was tempted to leave without another word.

Standing up, she looked down at me—a position that put me at even more of a disadvantage than I felt already. The scruffy, bumbling amateur detective facing a poised, competent, dominant member of the legitimate force. Struggling with my annoyance at this woman, I stayed seated, speculating that if she was on as much of a power trip as she appeared to be, it probably arose out of insecurity, and the more powerful I could make her feel, the better my chances were of getting a friendly reaction.

Gritting my teeth, I stared meekly up at her.

"People like you," she said dismissively, "make my job harder. If this were a murder, which it wasn't, you would be getting in my way and putting yourself in danger. I need to ask you to leave this sort of work to those of us who have been trained to do it." Having delivered the reprimand, she seemed to unbend a trace. "This wasn't a murder, Dr. McCarthy. But because it was an unexpected death, I did the routine checks. Casey Brooks had no money to speak of. Less than five thousand dollars in a savings account and a five-year-old Chevy truck were his only assets. Both were left to his mother, who lives in Las Vegas and was known to be there on the day he died. He has no other close relatives—no siblings, no ex-wife, his father's dead—and no one stands to gain in any way by his death."

"Except possibly the people I've talked about," I interjected.

"It's possible." She gazed at me cooly. "But not likely, I'm afraid. Once again: amateurs meddling in investigations only cause trouble. I'll thank you to leave this alone."

She turned with a decisive click of a classy black pump on the hard tile floor, and left me staring at the remains of my dinner. Detective Ward had, figuratively speaking, told me where to go.

She had also, I realized a minute later, told me part, at least, of what I'd wanted to know. There were no other significant suspects. Casey had not been killed for his fortune, or by some unknown ex-wife or brother or sister. If he'd been killed, in all likelihood it was one of the people I was "investigating," albeit in my amateur way. All that remained now was to work on alibis.

I was wondering just how I could start checking the various suspects' alibis as I headed through the parking lot toward my truck, when my pager started beeping once again. Muttering, I turned back to the restaurant and called the answering service from a pay phone near the door.

"This is Dr. McCarthy."

A woman's voice told me, "I have the fire chief on the line. He needs to speak to a veterinarian immediately. They have an emergency."

Slightly startled at the idea of a fire chief and contemplating various horrific scenarios in my mind, I said, "Put him on."

The man's voice was bluff, confident. "Gene Borba here.

We've got a horse trailer off the road, Doc. Came unhitched as the gal pulled off the freeway onto the Corralitos exit ramp. Rolled into a little gully and turned over. It's lying there now. There's a horse inside and it's still alive; it's thrashing around. Can you come?"

"Right away," I told him.

SEVENTEEN

I had no trouble finding the capsized horse trailer. The Corralitos exit was a scene of full-blown disaster—a mass of loudly flashing lights, red, yellow and blue, emergency vehicles, and of all things, television cameras. I didn't stop to ask how they'd gotten there, but as I hurried up to the man pointed out to me as Gene Borba, I heard a murmur of, "That's the vet," and several of the cameras swiveled my way. Oh great. My less-than-professional appearance would now be scrutinized by the entire county.

Clutching a syringe with three cc's of rompin in it, I asked, "Where's the horse?"

Gene Borba, a plump fiftyish man with a relaxed air in the midst of pandemonium, pointed his hand at a trailer lying upside down in the gully, wheels in the air; I could hear a sudden metallic banging from inside. Scrambling down the hill in that direction, I told a weeping girl who was clearly the owner, "I'm a vet. We need to tranquilize your horse so it doesn't hurt itself."

"Yes, please." Tears were running down her face. "Get her out of there, oh please."

The horse trailer was lying at an odd angle, but, by opening one of the small cupboard-like doors that allowed access to the manger so that one could feed and tie the horse, and then wriggling half my body inside, I was able to reach the mare, a little gray Appaloosa, lying on her side on what was supposed to be the roof, her whole head and shoulders wedged uncomfortably into the manger compartment.

"Hang onto my legs," I told a young man in uniform, "and if I say 'pull,' pull me out of here, fast."

Reaching as far in as I dared, I touched the mare's neck and talked to her soothingly. If she started thrashing now, I was in real trouble; one of her front feet could get me in the chest or face without any effort. I talked to her quietly, gritted my teeth, and poked the needle into her jugular vein, hoping I'd aimed well. Drops of blood welled reassuringly out of the end of the needle—I'd gotten the vein. Mercifully the horse was holding still and I injected the rompin slowly and carefully.

"Okay, pull me out easy," I told the hands holding my legs.

Once I was outside again, the sedated horse now quiet in the trailer, we held a conference. The fire chief wanted to dismantle the whole undercarriage of the trailer, cut it open, and lift the horse out with a crane. I pointed out that it was probably a poor risk to try lifting the horse through an opening like that, as her legs could easily be injured on the jagged edges of the cut metal. Watching a four-wheel-drive tow truck that had maneuvered its way into the gully and was sitting next to the trailer, all its lights flashing, I suggested diffidently to the chief that maybe the tow truck could manage to spin the trailer around so that its back doors were facing up and out, so to speak, rather than downhill and away from us.

"What then?" Gene Borba's voice was questioning,

open-minded; he clearly didn't know what to do and would welcome being told.

"If we could open both the back doors and cut the center divider out with a hacksaw so it was flush, we could hobble the horse's back legs together and let the tow truck pull it out of the trailer. Half the problem is the horse is more or less stuck in the manger. It can't get up."

The woman, girl, who owned the horse—she was twenty or so—erupted into fresh sobs at this point; the stress of the whole situation seemed to be too much for her.

I put a hand on her arm gently, trying to comfort. "I think we'll get her out of here okay. She looked fine when I gave her the tranquilizer—no injuries at all."

Wet eyes met mine with a desperate plea. "Do you really think she'll be okay?"

Nodding affirmatively, I said, "I stumbled on a trailer wreck like this when I was a graduate student. It looked much worse; there were two horses and one of them had tangled his legs in the manger and torn them up, and he was on top of the other one and looked as though he would trample him to death. But we got them both out and they were okay. The owner called me several months later to tell me they'd made a complete recovery."

The girl gave me a tentative smile and I smiled back. Tow truck attendants were in the process of hooking up machinery to the trailer—Gene Borba appeared to have accepted my idea. There was no crashing from inside; the horse still seemed to be adequately sedated.

I looked back at the girl. "I'm Dr. McCarthy," I told her. "I work for Jim Leonard—Santa Cruz Equine Practice."

She was young and scared, deeply unsure of herself. Hesitating, as if not knowing what to say, she ended up by staring down and mumbling, "My name's Jenny. Jenny Rogers. I don't have very much money. I borrowed this trailer to move my horse; I'm afraid I didn't hook it up right. How much will I owe you?"

I looked at the bent head of light-brown curls. "Don't worry too much about that. We'll arrange this so you can afford it. Let's just get your horse out, okay?"

I could hear Jim's irate voice in the back of my mind telling me not to be such a soft touch, but I ignored it. "You can pay the office what you can afford, in installments if you need to. I should go down there now," I added, seeing that various uniformed men were advancing on the trailer with hacksaws. "Make sure they don't hurt your horse."

She nodded, tears clearly not far from the surface. "Take care of her," she whispered.

"I will." I smiled again—my best reassuring smile—collected a syringe with more rompin in it and filled one with 10 cc's of ketamine, a drug which would knock the mare out cold for fifteen minutes or so. I wasn't sure if it would be necessary, but I wanted to be prepared. If the mare was frightened enough, rompin might not keep her quiet while we pulled her out, and if she struggled too violently she could hurt herself.

Dusk was filling the gully with shadows as I scrambled through the brush around the trailer. The tow truck's emergency lights flashed blue, yellow and red repetitively in the half-darkness, then were overwhelmed by a dazzling flood of switched-on white light from a press vehicle which had managed to worm its way up the gully. Various big, black cameras pointed toward the group of us around the trailer; firemen were sawing the doors off as I wiggled into the manger compartment one more time and gave the mare another cc of rompin, hoping she wouldn't get frightened and start struggling so that I'd have to put her all the way out.

She didn't. She lay still and remarkably quiet through the whole procedure, her head and shoulders still wedged in the manger compartment, her body resting on what was meant to be the ceiling but was now the floor. A fireman commented that it was surprising she would be so quiet and I smiled politely at him and didn't try to explain. In my experience horses who were trapped did one of two things: struggle until something snapped, often a part of their bodies, or wait quietly with what seemed almost human understanding to be helped. This mare was in the latter category—of course, the rompin probably wasn't doing any harm.

Rescue, when it came, was relatively uneventful. Using a long, soft cotton rope I kept in my truck for unsticking horses who had gotten cast in their stalls (rolled over so their legs were against a wall or through rails and they couldn't get up), we made an impromptu lariat loop which we put around the mare's back legs. This was attached to the tow truck chain, and while I watched the horse closely, the tow truck pulled her slowly and inexorably until, with a slight struggle, she came free of the manger and was able to scramble to her feet.

Squeals of joy came from the girl, who hugged the mare around the neck as she emerged from the trailer, television cameras snapping away at the pair of them. I checked the horse over carefully as a matter of routine; barring a few minor scrapes, she truly seemed to be fine. After making sure that arrangements were in progress to haul the animal to its new home, I gave the girl my card, took her number and departed, anxious not to be cornered by any television types for an interview.

Back in my truck with that adrenaline-wired feeling of wide-awake energy emergencies often gave me, the thought of going home and to bed seemed unappealing. It was eight o'clock, and dusk was just turning to darkness; the western sky, above rolling hills, showed a strip of still-glowing peacock green—all else was blue-black. Since I was halfway to

Watsonville I resolved to go see Melissa, the obvious next step in my "investigation."

When I pulled into her driveway, the mobile was dark, no cars in sight. No lights showed in Ken Resavich's windows, either, no white Cadillac by the house. Indian Gulch Ranch was silent under the night sky, apparently abandoned.

I got out of the truck and stared at the front door in the glow of the headlights. Now was the time, if I was ever to find out something useful. Overcoming my scruples, I knocked, tried the handle, and finding it unlocked, opened the door, calling "Melissa." No answer. I reached my hand inside and turned on the lights.

Neat and tidy, the room looked peacefully ordinary. Should I or shouldn't I? Still feeling indecisive, I went back to the pickup and shut off the headlights, then stepped into the mobile. Now, I told myself firmly, now is your chance to learn something.

As I stared around at the short beige carpet and the rental-unit furniture, feeling uncomfortably like a burglar, I wondered what in the world I'd say if Melissa walked in. That I'd stopped by to see her and wanted to leave a note, I decided. First step, write the note.

I walked over to the kitchen table, looking for paper and pen, and found them all laid out; Melissa had been paying bills. On top of the stack was a torn piece of paper. In large, round, schoolgirlish handwriting, as curvy as Melissa herself, were the words, "I'm taking Casey's truck and leaving town. I'm not sure where I'll go. Maybe Oregon. Maybe Texas. I'm going to find a job with another cutting horse trainer and start a new life. Don't worry about me. I'll be fine. Love, Melissa."

Staring at the scrap of paper, apparently written hastily and torn from the page, I wondered for whom it was meant. Surely not Ken. Not with that "Love, Melissa."

It was undoubtedly Melissa's handwriting; the same curling script appeared on the bills, and on a grocery list stuck to the refrigerator. I gazed around the room in consternation. Had Melissa left town already, or was she merely gone for the evening?

It proved surprisingly difficult to decide. The house was neat, but not scrubbed; there was food in the refrigerator, trash in the basket, bills on the table. There were also clothes in the closet and cosmetics in the bathroom, but less of each than I would have expected. All in all, I didn't *think* Melissa was gone for good, but I couldn't be sure. If she'd left in a hurry, traveling light, the place might look like this. If she had, she'd stolen Casey's pickup truck, which rightfully belonged to his mother, according to Detective Ward.

I found a small stack of clothes in a neat pile at the end of the couch, as if Melissa had decided she didn't need them at the last moment. As I looked at them I noticed the tape case behind them—"West Coast Futurity Finals," it said. The tape, I thought, that Casey had watched. I checked the VCR. Sure enough, there was a tape inside. Hesitating a moment, I turned the thing on, fiddled with the controls, and the picture jumped onto the TV screen.

A bay gelding working a cow in front of the herd, leaping back and forth, body in a half crouch, head down and stretched forward to the cow, front feet pattering—a dancing horse. On his back, instantly recognizable with his characteristic plain straw hat and simple blue shirt, silver-gray hair and quiet demeanor, sat Will George, looking focused and professionally intent.

Gus. Or the horse that was supposed to be Gus, winning the West Coast Futurity. The tape had apparently been wound to this spot. Had Casey, I wondered, watched Gus' run over and over again, becoming progressively surer that it wasn't the right horse?

Watching, I could tell only that the colt was having a terrific work. It looked like the bay horse in Will George's barn, but it might not have been. Casey would have known. Periodically the camera would zoom in on the horse's face, showing him in close-up. I could tell, for instance, that the horse wasn't Burt, whom I knew. This horse was the same color and there were no obvious distinguishing characteristics, but it wasn't the same face. Horses were like people, once you got to know them—all individuals, all different. Up close, it was hard to mistake a horse you knew well.

I watched the whole run, but didn't learn much. Will George marked a 76 to lots of noisy cheering. As he rode out of the ring I noticed that his help—the two herd holders and two turnback men who controlled the cattle while he worked—were Jay Holley, Dave Allison, and a couple of people I didn't recognize, one of them a woman.

Switching the tape off, I walked into the kitchen and looked at the bills on the table. Not very many. Power, garbage, phone. Checking the dates, I realized Melissa must have gone down to pick them up yesterday—getting the totals of what she owed, I thought, so she could pay them and leave. Why hadn't she paid them, then? Had she left that suddenly, afraid that a murder investigation would turn her way?

A sudden unsettling picture pricked at me, triggered by the memory of Lonny's words—"I'll pick the girlfriend every time." Melissa, standing in the doorway, not girlish or affected, as I had known her, but poised, quiet, and intent, pointing the business end of a gun at me. Melissa, with a dead-level tone in her voice, saying, "Gail, what are you doing here?"

I shivered, staring at the front door, then shook my head abruptly. It just didn't make sense. Melissa had no real motive to murder Casey. If she couldn't stand him anymore, she could just move out. Why kill him?

I stared down at the table, looking at the bills. Melissa had gone to the trouble of picking these up; she was probably planning on paying them. That meant she was out for dinner and would be back. I decided to wait for her and pretend I'd just been here a few minutes when she arrived. I needed to talk to Melissa.

Picking up the phone bill, I ran my eyes over it and the list of long-distance numbers caught my eye. I checked the dates. The last seven numbers had been called the night before Casey was killed, the night Melissa had said he'd "called a dozen people."

My breath caught sharply in my throat. Here, right here in front of me, could be the answer to the puzzle. It must have been one of these phone calls that had gotten Casey killed. He'd said the wrong thing to the wrong person, thrown a stone in a wasps' nest, and the wasps had come out in force. Or maybe just one wasp. A killer wasp.

Somewhere on this list . . . I picked up the phone from the table and started dialing.

EIGHTEEN

The first number proved to be Martha Welch. Her "hello" sounded clipped but familiar, and after an awkward second I placed the voice.

"Hi. This is Gail McCarthy. The vet who stitched up your mare."

"Oh. Hello." Her tone was not particularly friendly.

For the life of me I couldn't think of any useful lies. Oh well. "Did Casey Brooks call you the night before he was killed?"

"He did, the bastard." Suppressed fury vibrated in her voice and something else, something I couldn't quite place. "I told you. He said I poisoned my own horse, said he was going to spread it around. I told him I'd fix him and I did. I called everybody I knew and told them what kind of baloney Casey was trying to pull."

The woman was virtually frothing at the mouth and her speech had that rambling, loose-edged quality of one who'd been drinking. Still, this was interesting information.

"Casey actually accused you of poisoning your own horse?" I prodded gently.

"Yes, he did. He told me he wanted me to do something for him, and when I said I wasn't having anything to do with him ever again, he threatened me. Said he'd tell everybody I poisoned my horse."

"What did he want you to do?"

"I don't know. I didn't listen to him. Why should I? He never did a thing for me. Just like all horse trainers. They never ride your horse and then they charge you an arm and a leg." The easy emotionalism of self-pity welled up behind her words.

"So you don't know what he wanted?"

"He just wanted to blackmail me, wanted more money. I hung up on him."

"Did he say he wanted money?" God, this was frustrating. At least she appeared to be looped enough not to register that my questions were out of line.

"No, he didn't say so. But I knew it. That's what they all want. Horse trainers. Whoever. They want my money."

Shit. I simply was not going to get anywhere with this woman. I wondered if she'd been drunk the night Casey'd called her, and guessed that she probably had. Somehow or other it was easy to picture her as a closet drinker, one who would be routinely sauced each evening.

"Well, thank you. I'll sign those forms on your horse." All I wanted now was to bring the conversation to a reasonably graceful end.

"You'd better. You'd damn well better. I'll sue Jim's butt."

"Not to worry," I said briskly. "They're as good as signed. Good night."

Whew. I hung up the phone and stared at it thoughtfully, picturing Casey having roughly the same experience and feelings. Whatever he'd wanted from Martha Welch, he hadn't got it. So, who had he tried next?

Jay Holley, it seemed. The second phone number on the

list produced a recording that announced I'd reached the Salinas River Ranch and said to leave a message. The voice was cheerful and upbeat and I had a sudden mental picture of cold blue eyes in a grinning pale face.

I hung up at the beep and consulted the phone bill. Casey had talked to Jay for about ten minutes. Well, I'd known that, more or less. Jay had told Bret, and later, me, about the call. But had he told the truth?

The next number was in the area code for the Central Valley. A cool, noncommittal female voice said a brief hello. I had no idea who it was.

Ad-libbing desperately, I kept my voice even cooler. "Hello, this is Detective Ward from the Santa Cruz County Sheriff's Department. I'm looking into the death of Casey Brooks and I need to ask you a few questions."

"Oh." The voice sounded surprised. "I heard Casey was killed, but I didn't know there was anything suspicious about it. Was it murder?"

"We don't know yet," I said, imitating Detective Ward's stern style. "Who am I speaking to, please?"

"Sandy Barnwell."

"We have information that Casey Brooks called this number the night before he was killed," I said pompously. "Could you explain your relationship with him and what you spoke about that night, please?"

Sandy Barnwell snorted. "My relationship with Casey? I didn't have one."

"You knew him?"

"Of course I knew him. Everybody in the cutting horse business knew Casey. He was a real good hand."

Mouthing the last sentence with her as she spoke it, I cut in, "You're in the cutting horse business?"

"I train horses—cutting horses, mostly. I thought you knew, or why would you call me?"

"Would you please tell me everything you know about

Casey Brooks, especially his last phone call to you?" The bureaucratic style—we don't answer questions, we ask them—was almost fun, I thought, if you were on the dishing-out rather than the receiving end.

"I don't know much." Sandy Barnwell's voice was crisp. I tried to conjure up a face to fit the voice, but nothing came to mind.

"I saw Casey at the shows, that was about it," she went on. "We said hello to each other. We weren't particularly friendly, mostly because of Will."

"Will George?"

"Yes." The voice sounded surprised again, having supposed total ignorance on my part by now. "Will's a good friend of mine; I started out working for him and he's helped me a lot. Will and Casey were in some kind of pissing contest, and Casey figured I'd take Will's part. Anyway, what he called me about was the colt that won the West Coast Futurity. He was interested in buying him for a client, he said."

Casey, I guessed, had done a bit of ad-libbing, too.

"He wanted to know what I knew about him," Sandy Barnwell went on, "which wasn't really anything. Casey said he called me because he saw the tape of the finals and saw I was turning back for Will."

Bingo. Now I could put a face to the name—the female turnback rider on the tape—dark blonde hair pulled back in a ponytail under a white straw hat, middle thirties, a face that had looked more than tough enough to compete with the boys and win. Sandy Barnwell.

"I couldn't tell him anything about the horse," she said, "but one of the kids that works for Will—Tammy Hart—has an aunt that rides with me. I gave Casey the aunt's phone number, told him to get Tammy's phone number from her."

Cutting horses were a small world, I thought; everybody

knew everybody else. Casey had counted on that when he'd started calling.

Sandy Barnwell had nothing more to add, and the next phone number proved to be the aunt, as I had expected. I gave her my Detective Ward imitation, which I was finding handy, and confirmed Tammy Hart's phone number—the next number on the list.

A male voice answered the phone. Yes, Tammy was at home. After a moment a young female voice came on the line with a tentative "Hello."

Launching into the Detective Ward spiel, I quickly reduced Tammy Hart's reticence into an overawed eagerness to cooperate. Yes, Casey had called her about the horse, yes, she knew the horse, yes, she'd told him who'd ridden it for Will. And yes, Will hadn't ridden the horse at all, that she knew of. He'd just gotten on it at the Futurity.

That was the gist of her information. Hanging up thoughtfully, I dialed the next number on the list. No answer. No one home. But there had, I saw, been someone home the night Casey had called. The bill showed three minutes' worth of conversation.

Dialing again, I got two rings and then a tape. "You've reached Will George." I hung up the phone. Casey, it seemed, had talked to Will for five minutes or so, according to the phone bill.

The last number got me another recording, which announced that I had reached R & R Enterprises and Resavich Farms and that they were closed at the moment. I listened to the beep which preceded the message portion of the tape and wondered why Casey had tried to call Ken at his business. The phone bill showed that in all probability Casey had gotten the message machine, too—only one minute's worth of phone time was spent. Why not call Ken at home?

Looking up from the bill, I stared at the blank, black

square of window glass, toward where I knew Ken's house sat, lightless in the night. Maybe Ken hadn't been home that evening, either.

A shiver rippled down my spine. Suddenly the blackness outside the window made me uneasy. There I sat in the light, framed for anyone to see who was out there, lurking. Who would be out there lurking, I admonished myself, but the answer was unfortunately easy. Whoever had killed Casey. And "whoever" had a face now. Or at least I thought so. I thought I knew what Casey knew, what had gotten him killed.

And it had never occurred to me, I realized, with my unease turning to genuine fear, that it could get me killed, too. Why in the world hadn't it struck me that if someone *had* killed Casey, that same someone would desperately want Casey's death to be left an accident, would *not* want any amateur detectives nosing around stirring things up.

Intentions of waiting for Melissa vanishing into thin air, I got up abruptly, almost lunging away from the suddenly ominous window. I made for the door at a half run, wanting out, wanting home, wanting safety. I wished desperately for my gun, which was in my house, in its locked drawer; I seldom carried it, and it had never occurred to me until this moment to be afraid of Casey's unknown assailant—to be honest, I had never, until now, been completely sure that Casey had been murdered.

Virtually holding my breath, I cautiously opened the door of the mobile. No sound, no motion, no car but my own truck in the driveway, illuminated faintly by the light pouring out of the living-room window. I headed toward it, looking over my shoulder every other step. No one. No hurrying footsteps. Nothing.

I scrambled into the cab, locked the doors behind me and let out a breath. Safe, so far. I longed for Blue's comforting presence, even if he would have been less than useful as a defense system, but he too was at home, left in his yard with its comfortable doghouse.

Smooth, reassuring engine noise as I turned the key; I relaxed a hair and pulled out of the driveway with my jangling nerves starting to quiet. Indian Gulch Ranch lay under somber, unrelieved blackness all around me. A moonless night—ideal cover for would-be assassins.

The thought made me drive faster, and I pulled out onto Spring Valley Road with a deep sigh of relief. I kept up the speed, heading down the long grade the locals called Guadalupe at a good, brisk fifty miles an hour, driving toward the lights of civilization, of help and safety.

Trouble, when it came, seemed at first innocuous—a steady clunking noise somewhere in the front of the truck. The noise persisted, and, fearing a flat, I pulled to the side of the road, cursing. I did *not* want to change a tire alone in the darkness. Not now. Not tonight.

A flashlight inspection revealed nothing. All the tires looked fine. I kicked them in turn; none was flat. Jumping back in the truck quickly, I thought that whatever it was would keep until I got to Watsonville.

Wrong. The clunking grew louder and I slowed to a cautious thirty—and suddenly things started happening fast.

The front end of the truck shook violently, and the right side seemed to drop out from under me. Barely a glimpse in the peripheral glow of the headlights, one of my wheels bounced toward the verge of the road, and the truck was sliding hard to the right. Gripping the steering wheel, I strained uselessly to correct it—dark trees flashed surrealistically by the windows. Another moment of violent, disconnected movement, like nothing so much as one of those whirling, eggbeater type rides at the county fair—too rapid for fear—and everything came to a halt with a loud, solid, bone-jerking crash.

For a long moment I wasn't sure of anything—where I was, if I was hurt, if I was upside-down or right-side-up. Gradually I realized the truck was tipped to the right at a sharp angle, just off the side of the road. I was still in the driver's seat, more or less, and looking out the passenger window I could see branches and part of the trunk of a largish pine tree, a pine tree that appeared to be preventing the truck from rolling down what I remembered as a long, steep hillside.

The thought galvanized me back to life. Wiggling my toes and fingers, then my arms and legs, I took brief stock. It looked as though my knee had gone through the dash. The windshield was shattered, and I had a cut on my forehead that was dripping blood down my face, but there was nothing else wrong with my body that I could tell.

The truck was another matter. The driver's side door was undamaged and opened easily to allow me to negotiate with some caution a considerable drop to ground level. Once out, I stood there on the shoulder of the road, staring. The truck had slammed into the pine tree half sideways, half straight, and the general effect had been to crumple and twist the front end and cab pretty completely. One headlight and the taillights still glowed, showing that the right-hand side of the pickup was a mass of mangled sheet metal. I could see that a low-growing, stubbed-off limb of the pine tree had shattered the windshield, and thanked God it hadn't been my head. The cut on my forehead, I thought, swiping at the blood with the back of my hand, was probably just from the flying glass.

Surprisingly I felt no pain at all, though the smashed hole in the dash indicated that my knee should be hurting like hell. Adrenaline is a very effective painkiller. I peered past the crumpled wreck of the truck to the dark void of steep hillside beyond, and wondered if my wheel was lying down there somewhere, hundreds of feet below. Wondered if my truck would have been lying next to it, in a considerably more crumpled state, if it weren't for the pine tree.

Strange thought. I felt disoriented, as if reality had suddenly shifted and changed under my feet; the world looked dreamlike. I'd felt much the same after the massive shock wave of the Loma Prieta earthquake; nothing seemed real. I was aware of the black night around me, the silence, a slight wind muttering in the branches of the pine tree that had saved my life. Spring Valley was not a well-traveled road, but someone, I thought vaguely, should come along. Surely I wouldn't have to walk to Watsonville.

With that dismal thought came the glow of headlights behind me, winding down the hill, and my heart lifted. I waved an arm hopefully and the vehicle obligingly slowed and pulled in. I was walking toward it when I recognized the truck.

In a sick rush all my fear returned; I remembered Casey Brooks and the thoughts that the crash had driven out of my mind and saw, in the glow of the headlights, that the figure getting out of the truck was carrying a tire iron. A helpful, normal-looking tire iron, suddenly spelling disaster.

A wild glance showed no other cars in sight. I turned to run, to put the truck between us, to dive into the scrub, to get away somehow, and knew with awful certainty that it was too late. Hard running footsteps behind me, a grunting breath—I jumped sideways desperately and felt something hit my head. There was a rushing in my ears, and blackness.

NINETEEN

I came to consciousness slowly. For a long time I was aware only of pain, and not of myself as a person, suffering it. Only an endless thudding pain, simple uninvolved reality. Everything was black.

A long, long time before pain in blackness resolved itself into where-am-I type consciousness. Finally, I knew that I was lying face down with my hands behind my back in an uncomfortable position. I tried to move them and couldn't do it. Slowly I realized they were tied together. As were my feet. More slow minutes passed while I figured out the absolute blackness was due to a blindfold over my eyes. There was a gag in my mouth. I was, in fact, tied up like a victim in a melodrama. I had no idea where.

Little by little I remembered what had led up to this situation, and the pounding pain in my head was gradually superseded by a heart-stopping anxiety. My assailant meant to kill me, I was sure of it. Why I hadn't been bashed on the head and left in my truck, I had no idea. My death, as even I could see, was clearly necessary.

Fighting to turn my thoughts away from that dry-mouthed, fearful certainty, I noticed dully that my face was pressed against something that prickled. I turned my head from side to side. The green, sweet smell was familiar. Alfalfa hay. I was lying on hay. That meant a barn, probably. With that thought, the little noises that I'd only been vaguely aware of resolved themselves into the occasional creak and rustle of an old building, probably full of rats. All else was quiet.

I listened a long time, straining to hear some other sound, but there was nothing. I was tied up in a hay barn, then, with no livestock in it, probably. I couldn't hear any activity going on anywhere around it, either.

But why? Why put me anywhere at all? Why not just kill me and leave me with the truck, a nice, simple accident victim.

Thinking about that took my mind off the pain in my head for a while. Time passed. I lay there and breathed in the smell of alfalfa. My head throbbed, drowning out the dull aches in various other parts of my body. I began to wonder just how long I was to be left like this. No one, surely, would abandon me this way to suffer until I died of starvation.

The thought of it prickled the hairs on the back of my neck in an onslaught of primitive dread. I would not, I told myself, lie here tamely and wait for it to happen. I would not. My mind whimpered that I hurt, that I was cold and impossibly tired and I felt completely helpless. That was no good.

Think, Gail.

Slowly and carefully I explored with my hands the rope that tied them together. Good strong nylon rope, securely knotted. The rope was not so tight that it cut into my wrists, but it was snug. Though I spent a long while trying, I couldn't wriggle or twist my hands out.

I gave it a rest. I was getting colder by the minute and

though the throbbing in my head was, if anything, becoming a little more bearable, the cold was intensifying the aches in my body. My arms and shoulders, particularly, were starting to angrily protest their uncomfortable position, and my knee was shouting at me.

I could not, I told myself fiercely, just lie here and wait to die. If I couldn't get my hands free, what *could* I do? I wondered if I could stand up. My feet were tied tightly, crossed at the ankles. I tried to get up on them, but every time I got farther than my knees I fell. The falls sent waves of pain like electric shocks to my already aching brain. Not good.

I could roll over, maybe. I tried it. By jerking and twisting I could flop over, all right, like a fish out of water. The pain it caused my shoulders and head and knee left me gasping.

Remembering the heavy blow that had landed on my skull, I wondered if I was concussed. Thought of the quiet and rest prescribed for concussions and decided it didn't much matter. I had to get out of here, wherever here was, if I was to have any future at all.

I rolled over again. And again. I began to sweat. The pain when I jerked and twisted and thumped against the ground grew in intensity. My shoulders screamed. My knee felt as big as a football. I rolled again, cursing steadily, finding words I never thought I'd have a use for.

After a dozen or so rolls I lay still. I didn't think I could face another one. My face was pressed into the alfalfa—sweet green dust in my nose. I ached and throbbed and started to shiver again. One thing about the rolling, it kept away the cold.

My mind drifted. Lonny—he was out of town. No reason for him to worry if he couldn't reach me. I was often out on call; he would simply assume that was the case. Bret would think I was with Lonny, if he noticed my absence at all. If, in fact, he was still staying at my house. No way of knowing.

My house. I thought of its simple comforts—warmth, food, a soft bed—and tears swam into my eyes. I would never undervalue those things again. That is if I lived through this, which seemed unlikely. No one, I faced the fact, would come looking for me tonight. If it was still tonight. I had no idea how long I'd been unconscious.

Gathering myself, I tensed my muscles. I would *not* give up. There was no point in giving up. I rolled. Rolling made my shoulders shriek, jerked my head into throbbing life. I bit the gag in my mouth and rolled again. Another thing about it, when I rolled I didn't worry about being killed; I hurt too much to worry.

I rolled again. Sometime, somewhere, I had to hit something. The wall of the barn, if I was right. A wall I could rub against. I was not, I could not be, on some endless plain of hay, in some eternal limbo. Eventually, I had to hit a wall. I rolled.

Another roll. And another. I had to rest. I lay and sweated and wondered if I had any more left in me. Wondered about strength and weakness. I'd always thought I was strong, but I'd never imagined facing a test like this. I didn't feel strong now; I felt weak and helpless. I longed for some Sir Galahad to gallop to my rescue like a maiden in a story. Unfortunately, I couldn't see that it was likely to happen. I had to find the strength to reach that wall. I rolled again.

I rolled five more times. On the fifth roll I hit the wall. I lay there with my cheek against it for a long time, not thinking at all.

Eventually the cold twitched my mind back in gear. The one who had left me here could be coming back any time. Now that I had the possible means at hand to save myself there was no excuse to lie waiting to be killed.

I rubbed the side of my face against the wall. Rough, splintery boards that caught on the cloth tied around my eyes. I needed something that would catch more. Wiggling along the wall, I kept rubbing at the boards. After a while, I found what I'd been looking for. A nice sharp nail sticking out of a board. It dragged at my blindfold when I rubbed against it.

I rubbed. Pushed. Pulled. Occasionally, I'd miss my aim or push too hard and drive splinters or the nail into my face. I kept rubbing and pushing. There was a warm feeling on my cheek.

Slowly one corner of the blindfold worked its way down, then another. I fought with it and scraped at it and it came free suddenly, slipping over my nose.

It took me a minute to realize it had come off because the darkness seemed as absolute without it as with it. I rolled my head around, but I couldn't make out any shapes. No sunlight or moonlight leaked into my prison. It had been a moonless night, I remembered, when I'd left Indian Gulch Ranch.

Was it even the same night? A sudden panic rushed over me. I had no idea—no way of telling. I could have been out cold for days; I could be anywhere. In a barn somewhere in Nevada, maybe. Was I even on the earth, was life, as I understood it, still the same?

With all my will, I forced my mind to quit blithering. Stay calm, I told myself, don't panic. How likely is it they have alfalfa hay on Mars?

The thought of the hay, something known and familiar in this frightening blackness, was comforting. I rubbed my nose into it, smelled the sweet, dusty, green smell and tried to ground myself in reality.

It was unnerving not to be able to see, now that the blindfold was off. I was still sure I was in a barn, but what barn and where?

I wondered how long I'd been here. It seemed like forever, but I guessed it might have been for as little as two or three hours. Somehow I *felt* it was the same night, though again I couldn't be sure. It had been about nine-thirty when I'd left Melissa's; it could be, say, midnight now. If that was right, there would be many more long, dark, cold hours before morning.

Or would my killer step through the door in five minutes?

The thought sent me to rubbing my bound wrists on the nail, but it was soon obvious I was making no progress. Since I couldn't think of any other productive thing, I set myself at getting the gag off the same way I'd gotten the blindfold off. It took a long time. I persisted.

By the time it finally came off I'd been tasting the warm rusty flavor of my blood for a while. Lying still for a second with the gag and blindfold loosely around my neck like scarves, I was aware of my knee aching. Then I started yelling.

At first it sounded like a feeble croak. I sucked more air into my lungs and did my best. "Help! I need help! Come here. Anybody!"

Even in the straits I was in, it was hard to do. I felt ridiculous. But it couldn't hurt, I reasoned, and might help. If my captor had left me gagged, it meant he wanted me quiet. Maybe there was someone, somewhere, within hearing distance, who might come to my aid.

I yelled for a long time, but eventually hope faded. No one answered; no one came. No response of any sort. The barn remained unrelentingly silent. Once, when I stopped to listen, I heard an owl hoot. That was it.

My spirits, which had risen a little, plummeted drastically. Once again tears rose in my eyes as I contemplated the hopelessness of my situation. Nobody was going to help me. I was going to die, I was sure of it.

Frantically I started yelling again. "Help! Please help!" I kept it up, near hysteria driving me.

It was when I stopped to draw a breath that I heard the noise. Bushes crackling, leaves crunching, an irregular crashing in the brush. My whole body tensed and froze and cold reason gripped my mind. Someone was out there. Should I yell again?

I listened intently. Crackle, crunch. Silence. Snap, rustle. Not very far away. Someone or something, I corrected myself. The noises were erratic, haphazard, not the steady tromp, tromp that would be more typical of a human being. Deer, probably—maybe cattle or horses, though I didn't think so. There was none of the thud, thud effect that their heavier bodies were apt to produce.

I tried a tentative "Help!" and all noise ceased for a moment. Then, once again, crackle, crash, as the creature moved through the scrub. I yelled some more, on general principles, but produced no other results. The barn was somewhere remote, then, or at least somewhere where there was brush around it, and deer.

Still, I wouldn't have been left gagged if noise didn't matter. It was an off chance, probably, but the only chance I could see. I began yelling again, forcing myself to shout, "Help! I need help!"

I stopped to listen and heard only silence. Even the deer seemed to have disappeared. I shouted again, listened, shouted, for what seemed like hours, but could have been only minutes. My voice grew sore and my shoulders and knee throbbed agonizingly. Finally I lay still, feeling beaten, my face pressed against the hay, my eyes staring unseeingly at the darkness.

You will not quit, I told myself silently. You will not quit. I opened my mouth to shout again and saw light. Faint, but growing steadily brighter, it came from across the barn, fitful and bouncing, flaring suddenly and then dimming, gradually illuminating an open archway in the barn wall, revealing itself as the round yellow beam of a flashlight.

Hope surged hard in me, followed instantly by fear. For a long moment I lay perfectly still, my eyes fixed on the doorway and the approaching light. Closer, closer, it bounced and jerked until a figure stepped into the barn. In the peripheral glow of the flashlight, I could see the gist of his features under his cowboy hat and my heart dropped to the pit of my stomach.

This, most assuredly, was not rescue. Helplessly I watched the flashlight beam sweep to a spot maybe fifty feet away from me; the spot, I imagined, where I'd been left. Finding nothing, the light combed the barn relentlessly, searching.

There was nowhere to hide, no way to move quickly. My heart pounded as if it would burst from my chest; I strained against my ropes and tried to fight down an intolerable panic. The light was approaching.

It touched my face, blinding me, and I heard a muttered grunt of satisfaction.

Desperately, praying someone else was somewhere around, I screamed, "Help! Come quick!" at the top of my voice.

No response but quick footsteps across the hay and a savage "Shut up, bitch." A boot connected with my jaw and my head seemed to explode.

For a second I saw stars, literally, stars of shocking pain. Blinking my eyes, I willed myself to stay conscious, and stared up at the man above me.

With a wide, mirthless grin, Dave Allison met my eyes. "Now we'll see about you, miss nosy veterinarian."

TWENTY

It was the face I'd been imagining since I finished my phone calls; my fearful mind pictured him with all the sharp clarity of high noon, though I could barely see him with the flashlight trained in my direction.

Faded hair and skin, belligerent eyes, the strong wiry body of a man in his fifties just starting to sag toward the slackness of old age. Dave Allison. The failed horse trainer.

He reached down and flipped me over roughly, checking to see if my arms and legs were still securely tied, and my very flesh recoiled from his touch, cringing like a sea anemone.

Apparently he was satisfied; shoving me back on my side, he set the flashlight on its end and fiddled with it until it shed a soft diffuse glow rather than a sharp beam—instant lantern. Putting down a pack of some sort that he carried over one arm, he turned back toward me and stared into my face.

"Well now, I guess you were a little too smart for your own good."

His expression terrified me. Sharp, eager malice. He was

pleased to see me tied up and miserable. It made him feel good.

Desperately I searched the barn for possibilities in the light of the lantern, but drew a blank. It was just an empty barn—no hay bales, no equipment, nothing. Only the loose chaff covering the floor, residue of the alfalfa hay that had once been stacked here. Virtually an endless plain of hay from my point of view on the ground, stretching maybe fifty feet to the wide open archway of the door. Bitterly I noted that I'd probably taken the longest possible route to a wall in my rolling.

Dave Allison prodded me with the toe of his boot. "Did you think you were gonna get me locked up?"

He was gloating. I could hardly believe it. Naked, savage pleasure was plain on his face. I'm not sure what I expected, but not this.

Steeling myself, I croaked, "I don't know what you're talking about. I don't even know who you are."

He kicked me in the ribs, hard enough to hurt, and grinned at the wince I couldn't hide. "Don't bullshit me. I know what you've been doing."

I was silent and he smiled in satisfaction. "And you're not going to be around to keep doing it. I got it all figured out." He looked happy.

His hole, I thought desperately, his hole. His pride. Keep him talking.

"Why do you need to kill me?" I tried to keep my voice calm.

"You think I was gonna wait around for you to ruin me? Old Dave's a little smarter than that. You're dead, you stupid bitch. You're not playing any more detective games with me."

He stood looking down at me, the phony good-old-boy mask completely gone. A weak, spiteful child looked out of the faded eyes, but a dangerous child. A child who could kill.

Fighting down my panic, I kept my tone conversational. "Pretty good scam you pulled off."

He couldn't resist the impulse to brag. "You're damn right. I just collected twenty thousand dollars, and you're not going to get in my way, honey."

Scared as I was, I resented the "honey" and the sneer in his voice, but I managed to trot out a wide-eyed look. "How'd you make it work?"

"Don't you know, with all your poking around?"

"I know Will George rode a ringer at the Futurity, and that you were the one who produced it. You rode the Gus horse for Will."

"Well, I'll be damned. You ain't as smart as I thought you were. Seeing as you'll be dead shortly, though, I'll tell you; Will had nothin' to do with it. Will ain't smart enough to plan a thing like this." Smug satisfaction in his voice.

He seemed to like bragging to me while I was tied up at his feet, beaten and helpless, so I kept it up. "How'd you do it?"

"It was easy. That Gus horse is a solid bay, not a white hair on him. I went back to Texas and found me a good old pony who could really work and looked a hell of a lot like the three-year-old. There were a couple of little things, sure; the old horse had a big scar on his chest, but I got a breast collar that mostly hid it. Will never even looked at the colt the whole time I had it; I knew he couldn't know the difference.

"See, Will didn't like Casey. I guess you knew that. He didn't want to ride a horse Casey trained, so he had me ride him and just got on him at the Futurity. He had no idea he was riding a ringer. Will was my dupe, all right. I put him on the old horse to ride at the Futurity and sent him back home with the three-year-old and he never knew the difference."

It was all too possible, I thought. Will would have had his hands full at the Futurity; he'd probably had upwards of a dozen horses to show, some of which he would have trained himself and been really interested in. He could easily have never looked twice at the horse called Gus.

"So Casey caught you?" I stared up at Dave Allison's still-grinning face.

"That goddamned Casey was a little prick. I was sure as shit *glad* to kill him, I can tell you. Bastard never did anything but try and make trouble for me. See where it got him."

I remembered Melissa saying that Casey had beat Dave up when he came to get the horse, and recalled Dave's almost taunting glances at Casey at the cutting. Casey had made a worse enemy than he knew.

Dave was rolling now, distracted from whatever his plans were for me, interested in boasting. "I'll tell you, this thing was my idea, all mine, from the very beginning. The horse business is full of crooks; everybody in it is trying to cheat everybody else. If you want to win, you've just got to be the smartest. I used to be an honest horse trainer and look what happened. I was starving. I never made any money. But I figured out how you *could* make money, and I waited. Waited for the right guy to come along." Dave laughed.

Despite my situation, I almost felt like laughing, too. Dave's view of the world. An innocent horse trainer, trying to make it in a crooked business and having to cheat to survive. No mention that you needed talent and a good horse and willingness to work hard. Dave had apparently wanted an easier system.

"So who was the right guy?" I encouraged him.

"None of your damn business."

The sudden savagery in his tone was startling, and I flinched away as though from a physical blow.

In his watery eyes pure enjoyment showed. He saw me, I could tell, simply as an enemy, a threat. He had no sense of me as a human being, no sense that he was wrong to do this. I would never reach him through appeals to his morals or his pity. The only thing that counted to him was Dave and if I was a danger to Dave he would eliminate me. My best hope was to keep him talking.

"How'd you kill Casey?"

"It was easy. That goddamned Casey called me on the phone, told me he knew I'd given Will a ringer to ride, said he knew why. Said he'd ruin me. Next thing I knew Will called me and said Casey was telling *him* the horse was a ringer. I smoothed Will down, but I knew I had to do something about Casey.

"I just drove up to that spot where you can see the whole ranch the next morning and waited. I've gathered cattle on that ranch a dozen times in the past year; I know all the trails. When I saw which way Casey was taking that roan mare, I zipped on down the hill and waited for him. Easiest thing in the world to brain him with a rock. I made good and sure he was dead before I left. End of my troubles."

Ducking away from the too-obvious glee he felt in the killing, I asked, "Why'd you poison the horses to begin with?"

"You ain't even figured that out. Well, I had my reasons. But I poisoned a few more of them just to bother that damn Casey. If I'd had any luck at all the fucking cinch I cut would have broken at the right time and killed him. Spared me a lot of trouble."

The childish cruelty in his voice was more frightening than any amount of heavy menace. I made another effort. "Come on, Dave, what'd I ever do to you? Let me go and I'll help you. A vet could be useful."

"I'm not so stupid, honey. You'd get me in the end. Now shut up if you don't want your pretty little face all bruised."

He turned away toward the bag he'd set down, and my mind spun uselessly. I needed something—a lever, a bribe—something to influence him.

I tried the only thing I could think of. "You won't get away with this. I told the cops what I know, and Melissa knows Will rode a ringer. She's the one that told me."

Dave didn't stop rooting in his bag. "I don't think you told the cops anything, honey, because I haven't heard from them. And I sure ain't worried about Melissa." He turned back to me with a wide grin. "Melissa's dead."

TWENTY-ONE

The shock of it froze me for a long moment. Somehow I believed him absolutely. Melissa was dead and he'd killed her.

"But why?" I finally blurted out. "She didn't suspect you. She wasn't even interested. She wouldn't have pursued it."

"Precautions." He was rummaging in the bag again, getting things out. "A smart man takes precautions and old Dave is no dummy. Who knows what Casey might have told her. I decided I didn't need her running around. Yep, I took care of her today. She's in that truck of his, deader than a stone, in the bottom of a canyon in the Lost Hills. With any luck it'll be spring before someone finds her. And if it's sooner, so what. She took off, like her note says—part of a letter she wrote to her sister, the dumb bitch—took a back road, and got in a wreck. Nobody'll think any different.

"I was just sneaking back up to her place to tidy it up, make it look more like she'd left for good, when I saw you poking around. I watched you; you were a sitting duck in that window, and I figured out soon enough what you were up to, so I loosened all the lug nuts on one of your wheels. If you'd bit the farm in that wreck it would have been no big deal, but since you didn't, I've got other plans for you. People are gonna notice when you're not at the office tomorrow morning. I've got a use for you."

My skin prickled at his words; my mouth felt dry. What was he getting out of the bag? What was he going to do?

I stared at the things he'd set out. My God. An ax, some split kindling, newspapers, a box of matches, lighter fluid and a fire extinguisher. Oh my God. He was going to set the barn on fire. I couldn't believe it. Had to believe it. I stared at the objects on the straw, as mesmerized as a mouse with a snake.

Dave was crinkling up the newspaper. My heart pounded. I could feel clammy sweat in my armpits. I was going to die. Be burned to death.

I found myself hoping he'd knock me out before he did it, and shuddered at the thought of the rushing blackness. The end. End of everything I'd ever known, everything I might have hoped for.

Images flashed into my mind. My parents—would I see them? Lonny—regret for what we would never have, now. Blue and Gunner—who would take care of them?

I wasn't ready to die, my mind screamed. I hadn't lived enough.

Stop it, I told myself fiercely. Think. My mind flopped like a jellyfish. Fear was unrelenting. Think. Think.

Twigs snapped somewhere outside the barn. For a second my heart leapt wildly in hope and I opened my mouth to yell. Crackle. Crunch. Silence. Deer, I thought, it's just the deer.

Dave was frozen by his pile of kindling, listening. Suddenly, he lunged across the barn and grabbed my hair. Pain shot through my scalp as he jerked my head back and forced the gag up in my mouth. I could smell his breath, feel the heat of his body. Rough stubby fingers jerked the scarf until it cut my lips, then tied it tight.

Crackle. Crash. Coming closer.

Dave stood, listening. I could see the uncertainty on his face. Picking up the flashlight, he adjusted the beam so it was narrow and focused rather than diffuse, and strode out of the barn, the light bobbing away with him.

Blackness reigned. Think. The objects that had come out of the bag. The objects that hadn't been there before. Suddenly, I knew what to do.

Visualizing the barn interior as accurately as I could, I flopped over, rolling toward where I remembered them as being. Not too far away. Maybe ten feet.

Flop. Roll. My face thudded into the hay. I felt no pain, only wrenching anxiety. Twisting, I searched with my face, brushed something hard, splintery. Wood.

The kindling. The ax was next to it. I wriggled, felt the edge of the ax blade with my face, twisted until my wrists were against it, and rubbed furiously, heedless of skin and blood.

Back and forth, back and forth, as much pressure as I could apply. I could feel the ax cutting the rope, but it was slow. Stay away, Dave, I prayed. Please stay away.

One piece of rope gave, then another. I jerked my wrists apart, sat up, grabbed the ax, and started working on my feet.

Too late. A faint light bobbed in the distance. Dave was coming back.

I sawed furiously at the ropes around my ankles. One gave, then another, and I pulled them off. I could see the round yellow circle of the flashlight beam. Too late to run, too late to ambush him as he walked in the door. Gripping the ax, I scrambled to my feet and almost fell.

Desperately I steadied myself. Took the half second remaining to bend my aching knee, take a deep breath, tighten my grip on the ax. I stood there, swaying slightly, but crouched and ready, with the ax poised over my shoulder like a batter, when Dave's light touched me.

In the glow, I could see his face fall in a way that would have been funny under any other circumstances. He'd expected me tied up and helpless; instead, he saw me free and wielding an ax.

He had a second of real doubt, I could tell, and my heart soared. If he'd been carrying a gun, surely he would simply have pulled it out and shot me. Instead, his face hardened into lines of resolve; he swung the heavy black truncheon of a flashlight over his shoulder in an imitation of my stance.

"Oh yeah," he grunted.

Balancing myself, I tried to be ready and let him make the first move.

He swung the flashlight at me in an obvious feint and I sidestepped. Realized how weak I was. Took a desperate grip on myself and waited for him to swing again.

He must have read my weakness because he came in fast and hard, swinging the flashlight at my face. I dodged and parried with the ax and he launched a savage kick at me. I saw it coming and got out of the way, but I nearly fell down doing it.

We faced off again, weaving and faking moves in the jerking flashlight beam, locked onto each other in a sick parody of a cutting horse on a cow.

This can't go on, I thought. I have to look for a spot to hit him and try and knock him out. I have to.

I waited for him to rush me again, but he caught me by surprise and threw the flashlight at me. Light and darkness swirled wildly and it hit me in one shoulder. I dropped the ax.

He started to come in on me with his fists, saw the ax fall, changed his mind and went for it. I had a split second to think. No use wrestling Dave for the ax; I hadn't a chance. I saw the fire extinguisher in the beam of the rolling flashlight and reached down for it.

I almost didn't come up. Dave had the ax and swung it at me in one fierce motion. I felt it coming and threw myself sideways. He missed me by a hair, but the violent jerk was too much for my fragile balance and I ended up on my side in the hay, clutching the fire extinguisher.

Dave was coming at me with the ax above his head and all his strength gathered for the downward swing. I aimed the fire extinguisher at him and pulled the trigger.

White powdery dust shot in his face, catching him totally by surprise. Some of it got in his eyes, and the ax came down to the left of me. I kept spraying it at him as well as I could, and struggled to my feet.

His coughs mingled with choked yells of "bitch" and the air between us was full of white chalky powder. I held my breath. He swung the ax savagely in all directions, unable to see, a major leaguer desperate for a grand slam.

He couldn't see, I thought. Timing it as well as I could, I waited until he was off balance, gathered myself and lunged in, kicking him in the groin.

He screamed, stumbled, went down. I grabbed the ax, hardly thinking, swung it over my shoulder and brought the flat side of it down on the back of his head, hard. He crumpled instantly. Dead or alive, I thought, you bastard, I don't care.

For a long second I stared at him, helpless and silent on the ground. Then I turned, picked up the flashlight, and started out of the barn.

TWENTY-TWO

Once outside, shock seemed to catch up with me. I had no idea where to go, no idea where I was. The flashlight showed a forest around me and a dirt road running off through the trees. I followed the road.

Thoughts, disconnected, disbelieving, swirled through my mind as I tromped along in the bobbing beam of light. The night was still and dark, moonless as far as I could tell in this tunnel of trees. From what Dave had said, I was pretty sure it was the same night.

Night from hell, I thought grimly. My knee throbbed painfully as adrenaline seeped out of my system; I felt weak and trembly all over. My leg muscles twitched. I kept walking. Eventually this road would lead somewhere. It had to.

It took a long time, or I thought so, anyway, but eventually the dirt road, muddy in patches from the recent rain, and impassable for anything but a four-wheel-drive vehicle, joined a paved road. There by the side, half hidden in a clump of trees, was a pickup. Dave's pickup. Hopefully I tried the door and found it unlocked.

Hope died a second later. Dave had taken the keys. I was

not, absolutely not, going to go back to the barn and look through his pockets. I would just keep walking. The question was, which way?

The paved road gave no hints. Narrow and unmarked, it boasted no road signs, no indications of any sort what it was or where it was. I could be anywhere in the world, as far as I knew.

No, that's not true, I told myself. It's the same night. I must be in central California somewhere; he couldn't have taken me much further away.

Central California is a big area. I stared up at the sky—what I could see of it through the trees. Some faint stars, but they didn't reveal anything to me. I needed to choose a direction. Dave might merely be out for a few minutes. If he came to, the first thing he'd do would be aim for his pickup.

The thought shoved me into motion. The road sloped slightly; I chose the downhill direction on the somewhat illogical grounds that one should always follow a creek downstream, if lost in the woods.

A road is not a creek, I told myself, but what the hell. I trudged. My feet were getting cold. My knee throbbed. I hoped and prayed the batteries in the flashlight were good and strong, wondered if maybe a car would come down the road.

None did. By my reckoning, it was at least three in the morning and the road had an untraveled look. Probably not much chance that someone would come along.

What seemed miles later, my road reached another, larger road. There was a gate and a mailbox; my road appeared to be a driveway. I swung the flashlight around. The gate, the mailbox, the whole entrance looked familiar. It took me a few seconds, but I got it. This was Martha Welch's driveway.

I'd been on Martha Welch's place then, in a barn on her property. The immense relief of knowing where I was swallowed up all questions as to why Dave had brought me here in particular. This was Mt. Madonna Road I was standing on. I knew which way to go.

I headed down the hill again, toward town, toward civilization. Casserly Store sat at the junction of Mt. Madonna Road and Casserly Road, and it had a pay phone in front of it. No matter that it was a mile away. At last I was back in the world I knew.

My elation vanished rapidly. It was still cold, and I was getting weaker and sorer by the moment.

I eyed the occasional houses I passed, but they were dark and quiet, all occupants asleep. Somehow the notion of knocking, waking them, my own appearance—gag and blindfold around my neck, dried blood on my face and wrists—seemed worse than walking. I kept walking.

Thoughts began to tromp through my mind to the rhythm of my footsteps. Panic had subsided; tiredness seemed to bring a clear head. Slowly I began to unravel the knot and make sense of some of the things Dave had said. One foot in front of the other. Conclusions followed inexorably. Thinking kept exhaustion at bay.

By the time I reached the Casserly Store, a half hour later, I was sure I understood how it had all happened and why.

Marching up to the phone, I punched in a number, then my card number, and waited. Three rings. Four. Five. Be there. Please be there.

On the eighth ring someone picked up and my heart soared in relief.

Grinning stupidly, I spoke into the receiver, "Bret, old buddy, I need help."

An hour later—4:00 A.M., actually—Bret and I sat in his pickup arguing. He'd come to fetch me immediately, brought what I'd requested and driven me where I'd asked to go, but he was balking now.

"Why don't we just call the sheriffs and let them take care of this?"

"Because." I stopped, stumped for an answer he would accept.

"Because why? Jesus, Gail, you look like death warmed over, you say you were knocked out and tied up and about to be burned to death by Dave Allison, who incidentally killed Casey and Melissa, and who is lying in a barn where you knocked him over the head, and you don't want to call the sheriffs?"

"Will you just listen to me! Do what I tell you. Let me out of this pickup and wait here for me. I am goddamn sure going to do this, with your help or without it." Bret was staring at me; I realized I was shouting. My hands were also trembling.

"You're in no state to go in there." His voice was soft.

I took a grip on myself. "I need to do this," I said as calmly as I could. "I don't trust the sheriffs to get it done. Tell you what. You go on down there," I waved a hand down the hill, "and call them as soon as I go in. Then come back here and wait for me."

Bret shook his head, but agreed reluctantly. "All right. And if I hear any noise, I'm coming in."

"You do that." I got out of the pickup, my heart thudding with fear despite my brave words, and walked slowly toward the house.

All was darkness. I knocked on the front door and waited. Everything quiet, no lights in the windows. I knocked again.

Despite the silent, deserted atmosphere, I was sure someone was there. Awake, I thought. Waiting, probably. Scared, maybe.

On the side of the house, some glass doors reflected the

faint starlight. I walked along the porch to them and looked in. Shapes of furniture loomed in a big room. With a sudden jolt, my brain registered a human shape in a chair near the window.

Closing my hand around the butt of the pistol in my jacket pocket, my .357, which Bret had brought me, I knocked on the glass.

The figure didn't move. I tried the door; it was unlocked. I opened it gently, but it still squeaked. The shape in the chair turned to face me.

Gripping the gun, I stared back. I could see eyes, that faint unmistakable liquid sparkle in the darkness of the face. Then the voice. "Is he dead?"

"I don't know," I said levelly. "Can I come in?"

With a sigh that could have been relief or defeat and a slight motion of his hand, Ken Resavich waved me into his living room.

TWENTY-THREE

He was sitting in a padded, basketlike chair in front of a wall of glass. The lights of Watsonville sparkled below, and distant glittering lights lined the curve of the bay. Ken's front room, like Martha's, had a view.

I spoke his name and he inclined his head toward a nearby chair and lifted his arm. My stomach muscles tightened, but the shiny thing in his hand was a drink.

"Have a seat," he said. Then he swiveled back toward the window.

I walked to the chair he'd indicated and sat, feeling awkward. This wasn't going quite as I'd expected.

Ken Resavich sipped his drink and stared out at the view. "You're not sure if he's dead," he said finally, not looking at me.

"I hit him over the head pretty hard. He tried to kill me." I spoke as neutrally as I could manage.

Ken sighed. "I've been waiting. Waiting to hear one way or another." His voice sounded tired, but the same. Unemotional, formal tones. His face, in the faint light from the window, was as expressionless as ever. Yet, he was facing ruin.

"Did you know," I said slowly, "that he was planning to kill me?"

He swung his chair back toward me. All my muscles contracted with a ripple, but when he spoke his voice was quiet, polite as ever. He didn't look threatening. Why did I keep waiting for the gun?

"I didn't know," he said. "But I suspected."

"He killed Casey; you knew that."

"Not to begin with. I wasn't sure, anyway. But I knew, later. He told me."

"Why? Why did you let him do all this?"

"I didn't." A long pause. "I didn't intend any of it."

I let the silence grow and after a while he spoke, slowly, picking and choosing his words, as if the right ones were difficult to find.

"I've always been a successful businessman. My father was a farmer and I inherited his land. I've made it produce, made it pay, ten times what he did. But . . . my father. You had to know my father.

"His father, my grandfather, was from Croatia, and my father had that sort of pride you sometimes see in the children of immigrants who've done well. He, my father, was a handsome man, a flamboyant man—he had a sports car, always kept a pretty mistress, and he loved horses. That old country-western song about faster horses, younger women, older whiskey, and more money was written about my father." Ken laughed—a dry chuckle.

"I was his only son and I never measured up. I was always quiet, and though I was good at school, it wasn't what he wanted. He died of a heart attack at fifty, just as I was getting out of college, and I know he thought of me as a failure. I never had the women or the sort of color he wanted me to have."

Ken took a long swallow of his drink and stared out into

the darkness over the bay. Faint, almost indistinguishable light marked the horizon to the east; dawn was coming.

"My father died twenty-five years ago, and I'm still trying to prove something to him. He had cutting horses, and when he died I didn't sell them, even though I've always been afraid of horses. My father rode them himself, but I hired other people to ride them and gradually I got the idea that I'd succeed in the cutting horse world, *his* world, in a way he never did."

I stared at Ken in fascination. His words painted a picture that was suddenly very vivid. "Where'd Dave come in?" I asked.

He looked at me with the faintest of smiles. "I wasn't winning. I won some here and there, but what I wanted, what I needed, was a great horse, one who would dominate the industry and make my name a legend."

The words, I thought, were full of emotion, but the voice and face were as wooden as ever.

"Dave came in because I was buying cattle from him. He was at the ranch one day when Casey was working my new colt—Casey called the horse Gus—and I told Dave I had hopes I'd win the Futurity with him. Dave laughed. Said I'd never win the Futurity with Casey, no matter how good the colt was. To make a long story short, Dave must have seen something in what I said—something that told him how much I wanted to win the Futurity.

"He called me a week later. Said he'd make sure I won it. He'd have Will ride the horse, he said. He had a plan. And he wanted a cut."

Ken sipped a little more of his drink. "He said I'd have to fork out a little extra money, of course. But it would all be completely safe.

"I knew what he was. I didn't ask him what his plan was—though in the end I figured it out. The extra money was to buy the other horse; Dave sold him afterwards and pocketed the proceeds, I think, on top of the ten thousand I gave him. But I had the money to spare.

"The one thing I wouldn't do was get rid of Casey, even though Dave wanted me to. Casey had talent, even I could see that. I thought in the end he might train some champions for me. I told Dave I'd sell the Gus horse, ostensibly. And I did. I sold him out of my name and put him in the name of one of my companies, R & R Enterprises. Casey didn't know anything about my business. I was pretty sure he wouldn't recognize the name if he ever saw it."

R & R Enterprises. The light clicked on in my brain. That last night, while he was making phone calls, Casey must have asked Will George who owned Gus. And Will, having no reason not to tell him, had said some company named R & R, and given him the phone number. Casey had called; I remembered the recording. "You have reached R & R Enterprises and Resavich Farms." Casey had known.

"Casey found out, didn't he?"

A long, long silence. Trees were black silhouettes on the eastern ridge—the sky blue-black behind them. The lights of Watsonville seemed faded.

"Yes, Casey found out. He came to this house, sat right where you're sitting and told me he wouldn't let me get away with it. I tried to buy him off but he wasn't interested. Said he'd think it over and decide what he had to do."

Casey, I thought, had signed his own death warrant.

Ken was still talking. "I called Dave; Casey had called him, too. Dave just said not to worry, he'd take care of it. Told me to be sure and be gone from the ranch the next day, be somewhere where people could see me all the time."

Ken's face turned toward me. In the dawn light, I could see him a little better, but I still couldn't read his feelings.

"He didn't tell me any more and I didn't ask. I didn't do anything special. I went to work, the way I always do, just made sure I stayed around the office all day. And that evening . . . well, you know. You told me."

"Dave killed Casey and made it look like an accident," I said matter-of-factly. "But you knew it wasn't an accident."

"I was pretty sure."

I remembered the gray look on his face when I'd told him; Ken had been sure all right. Casey—all that brilliant life and talent—had been snuffed out to protect Ken and Dave's scam, and Ken knew it.

"Just to win the Futurity?" I said it bitterly, and it prompted the strongest response out of Ken so far.

"Not *just* the Futurity," he snapped. "Gus was a stallion. And he was a good colt. I thought that if he had the Futurity win on his record, and Will George showed him successfully for a few years, he could go on and stand at stud and become a legend."

Vindicating Ken to his long-dead father, I added to myself. "So you didn't intend to run any more ringers?" was what I said.

"No."

"I'll bet Dave did."

Ken shook his head slowly. "I don't know what Dave thought he was going to do. Dave was out of control. And now you tell me he's tried to kill you. I didn't intend . . . any of that."

A long, heavy silence. I thought of lots of things to say along the lines that Ken's passivity had done every bit as much damage as Dave's power-hungry maliciousness, but kept my mouth shut in the end. He'd either see it for himself or he wouldn't.

"There's one thing," I said slowly, "that I don't understand. The thing that started all this. Why did Dave poison the horses to begin with?"

Ken laughed, a short bark of a laugh with an edge to it.

"Because of something I said one day when he was over here picking up cattle. I told him I had two horses that hadn't panned out; I'd never be able to sell them for what they were worth. He asked me if they were insured and I said yes. Then he asked me to point them out to him. He said if I collected on them he wanted twenty-five percent."

"And you didn't ask him what he meant to do?"

"No."

Ken's horses, not Martha's. I'd never made the connection. The insurance companies had been in touch with me about *Ken's* horses, and I'd thought nothing of it. Many, if not most, valuable show horses were insured. Casey'd never thought of it, either.

"It was sheer bad luck that Martha Welch's horse died and she made such a fuss about it." Ken sounded resigned.

"Bad luck that Dave poisoned eight horses for no reason at all?"

"I told you; I couldn't control him. I had no idea he was going to poison mine, let alone any others. And I couldn't do anything about it, even if I'd wanted to. He could blow the whistle on me for fraud. If I took him down I was going with him."

There was genuine emotion in that statement. Going down, losing, failing. That had been intolerable to Ken. And now?

He looked at me. In the growing light I could see his eyes seeking mine. "You'll turn me in," he said. "You have to." It was a statement of fact, said without emphasis, as close to a plea as he would ever get.

I matched his tone. "You're right. I wanted to see you first. It's personal with me. Dave tried to kill me, I told you that. I needed to know if that was your idea, too."

"No." He said it decisively. "Whatever I wanted, I had no intention of killing anyone."

We stared at each other in the soft gray light of dawn, our

faces mutually drained and sad. I believed him. No matter that I thought his essential lack of force had been the catalyst that set Dave loose. It was Ken's money and his passive, cowardly willingness to cheat that had made it possible for Dave to do what he did.

"So where is Dave?" Ken said it heavily, as if he really didn't want to know.

Even so, my survival instincts prickled. If Ken could find Dave and make sure he was dead, it would simply be my word against his on all these things.

"I'm not sure exactly," I lied. "In a barn somewhere."

"And you hit him over the head and don't know if he's dead or alive."

I was silent, thinking it had not been my smartest move to reveal that Dave might already be dead. Ken had everything to lose. If luck just fell his way, if Dave was even now food for worms, there was no one but me left to eliminate. That was how it would look to him, anyway.

The thought seemed to cross his mind. He stared at me steadily, then reached into the soft depths of the basket chair and brought up the gun. A short, businesslike pistol with a silvery sheen. My stomach muscles contracted in earnest and I gripped the gun in my own pocket, pointing it at Ken through the thin fabric. Now what?

"I've got a gun," I croaked. "In my pocket. It's pointed at you now."

Ken looked at me as if he didn't believe me and I wondered if I'd have to shoot him. My heart thumped hard, and I willed my face to stay quiet. Despite the rush of fear I felt surprisingly detached. If he points that gun at me I will shoot him, I told myself firmly, adjusting my gun so it was trained roughly at the center of his body.

Ken held his own gun idly, not pointed at me, but not pointed a long way from me either. He didn't seem worried about my threat; in fact, he didn't seem very aware of me, lost in some train of thought of his own.

It was all surreal. The dark room, dawn waking in the windows, Ken's expressionless face. I felt like a character in a play. I was afraid all right, but nothing like the fear I'd felt with Dave. Maybe I had just been through too much. I faced Ken quietly, aware of my thumping heart, but calmly planning what I would do if the round black hole of the gun swiveled my way. If I live through this, I thought, I will have gotten an awful lot of practice in how to stare down death. More than I ever wanted.

As idly as he had picked it up, Ken let the gun drop back into the cushiony seat of the chair. My stomach muscles relaxed a fraction.

"It's loaded," he said quietly, his face and voice as colorless as ever. "I thought for a while I would shoot myself with it. A minute ago, I thought I might shoot you."

It was strange to hear him speaking of killing in such uninflected tones. It was as though he'd divorced himself from his emotions, discarded anything in his personality reminiscent of his colorful, flamboyant father. A sort of self-defense, maybe. Even now, with the end of all he'd worked for in sight and a gun in his hand, he sounded unaffected.

"I've always played to win," he said. "And the more I think about it the more I think I wouldn't win by killing you. I haven't murdered anyone. The most I could be charged with, besides fraud, is being an accessory to murder. It makes a lot more sense to hire a lawyer and buy my way out as well as I can. I've got the money."

He did at that. For a long moment we stared at each other, some sort of unspoken message passing; at the same time I became aware of the distant whine of sirens. Ken heard them, too.

"I called them," I said bluntly. "They're coming." And thank you, Bret, I added silently.

I still wondered if he might pull out the gun in some futile, last-ditch effort, but he seemed to have no such inclination. He watched me quietly as the sirens grew louder, thinking his own thoughts.

When the noise filled our ears and the tires scrunched on the gravel driveway, he offered one final comment.

"I'm sorry about Casey. He was everything I couldn't be—everything my father wanted."

"Yeah," I said slowly, "he was a real good hand."

TWENTY-FOUR

Three days later I was brushing Gunner as Lonny leaned on the fence, watching me. He'd arrived back from the mountains early that morning and called me at work, and I'd made a date to meet him here at five o'clock.

Rehashing the story of how I'd acquired Gunner, and my hopes and fears about owning him, as I brushed his warm red coat, just starting to turn thick and fluffy in time for the approaching winter season, I could sense Lonny's puzzled impatience.

"So, I'm not sure what I'm going to do with him now that Casey's . . . dead," I finished lamely.

"Gail, what happened?" Lonny was direct, as always. "You haven't said a word about it, but I read in the newspaper this morning that Dave Allison was arrested for the murder of Casey Brooks and Melissa Waters, and Ken Resavich is accused as an accessory. I never saw your name, but I know you were involved somehow."

"How do you know?"

Lonny grinned. "The amount of trouble you were getting up to, it was inevitable. Now give."

I picked up the comb and began working on Gunner's mane, untangling the long, coarse black hair and combing it until it ran through my fingers easily.

"It's a long story," I told Lonny, my eyes on the mane, "and some of it is kind of hard for me to tell."

"So begin at the beginning and go to the end. After I left that morning . . . ," Lonny prompted.

"Okay. After you left . . . ," I began. Slowly but steadily I recounted events as they'd happened, glossing over my terror in the barn as much as possible. By the time I was done, Gunner's mane and tail were combed, silky waterfalls of shiny black hair.

Lonny was quiet; he'd said little the whole time, but lines of concern framed his green eyes. When he spoke his voice was serious. "I wish you'd called me."

"When was I supposed to? When I was tied up in the barn? I'd damn sure have called you then if I could."

"Before. After. The next day. Any time."

I sighed. "Lonny, this could be a problem. I appreciate your concern, I really do, but remember when you asked me if I was free and I told you I wasn't sure if I wanted a relationship? Well, this is what I mean. I'm used to taking care of myself, and I'm *not* used to checking in with somebody."

Lonny's face was grave, but after a minute he nodded slightly. "All right. Accepted. Let me ask you a question. Why in the hell did he put you in Martha Welch's old hay barn?"

Relieved at a return to the facts, I said, "I'm not sure. He was still lying there, concussed, when I brought the sheriffs—all the paraphernalia he had to tie me up and light the barn on fire right next to him—so they had no trouble believing my story. But Jeri Ward questioned him for hours after he came to and he wouldn't say anything, or so she told me."

Lonny grinned. "So it's 'Jeri' now?"

I smiled back. "Well, she didn't exactly invite me to call her by her first name and I still think she thinks I'm a royal pain in the ass, but we have spent quite a little bit of time together in the last couple of days. I more or less suggested she keep my name out of things in exchange for my giving her all the information I'd come up with and she was pretty ready to buy that. You'll notice she gets the credit for solving the case in those newspaper articles."

"Yeah, I noticed."

"That was our deal. When I signed my statement, she agreed to keep me out of it. As far as Martha Welch's barn is concerned, my theory is that Dave meant to pin my murder and maybe even Casey's on Martha.

"Martha was at home that night and drunk; I know, I called her. Dave may have done the same. He was her resident hired trainer several years ago; Jeri Ward found that out by questioning Martha, who, as you might expect, was furious. Dave knew all about her place, apparently, knew where that old hay barn in the back pasture was, knew it wasn't used anymore. He also knew Martha had a motive for murdering Casey."

"You mean that squabble they were having over the horse that died?"

"The horse that Dave poisoned. Right. Dave poisoned Ken's two horses to get the insurance money for them, and poisoned a few more to make it look as though they weren't a particular target if anybody was nosy. I'm sure he thought it all would be put down to bad hay. Which it would have been. Except for Casey."

"So it was just bad luck, or good luck, depending on how you look at it, that Martha's horse died?"

"I would guess so. Dave probably gave Ken's horses whopping great doses, and the other horses less. Martha's horse just twisted a gut and it did him in." I shuddered. "I just can't imagine how anyone, any horse person, anyway, could do that."

Dave's face jumped into my mind, that weathered, outdoor face, not unlike the face of any fiftyish rancher. Dave had spent his life around horses, as I had, devoted what time and talent he had to the big, graceful, gallant creatures. What would make such a fundamental difference between us?

The need for power, I supposed, that time-honored human weakness. Power over others, status, the trappings of wealth—all seen as an antidote to some sort of self-perceived lacking. Dave's failure as a trainer had bitten deep, perhaps, corroded away his sense of himself.

"It's hard to understand," Lonny murmured. "A hard question to solve. The nature of evil."

"Yeah. Dave was evil, as I read evil. He wasn't aware of anyone or anything as having feelings or needs except Dave. And he was so anxious for power, control, wealth, whatever you want to call it, that he was willing to destroy people, and horses, by the dozen. I call that evil."

"What about Ken?"

"I don't know what to think about Ken. That was a strange encounter."

I remembered the dark room, Ken's quiet words, the sense I'd had that he was being honest with me. "Ken's failure was in being passive, in letting Dave's evil have its way. I'm not sure how I feel about that. There's no denying he bears a lot of responsibility. He could have stopped Dave just by refusing to go along."

Ken's passivity, I thought, was a response to his father's aggressively dominant personality. Still, that neither excused nor absolved his behavior, though it might explain it.

No psychological justifications could ever ameliorate the grievous harm he'd done.

"Do you think old Will knew he was riding a ringer?" Lonny asked.

"I don't know," I shook my head. "You'd think he'd know; he's probably ridden hundreds of cutting horses. I'd guess a solid older horse would feel different to him than a three-year-old, no matter how good the three-year-old was supposed to be."

"You'd think there would at least be a question in his mind."

"Maybe he didn't want to ask any questions. He won the Futurity, after all." My mind pictured Will George's serene blue-eyed face. "Maybe he suspected and just didn't care."

Picking Gunner's feet up one by one, I dug the packed-in dirt out of the bottoms with the metal hoof pick, cleaning the pads called frogs, scraping until the soles and fissures were bare. No thrush, no rot, no infections. Nice, healthy feet.

I stood up and patted his shoulder. "I don't know exactly what I'm going to do with you, fella."

Lonny smiled. "Let's make a rope horse out of him. He's big enough."

That was true. Gunner was already 15.2 hands, big for a three-year-old.

"I don't know how to train a rope horse, any more than I know how to train a cutting horse," I pointed out.

"I do. I'll help you. He looks like a nice colt, and if Casey Brooks liked him, that's good enough for me."

"But I don't know how to rope."

"I'll teach you." Lonny smiled again, that open, infectious smile. "Burt's a babysitter. He'll take care of you."

"All right." I smiled back at Lonny and felt, for the

first time since what I thought of as 'that night,' full of hope.

"How about tonight?" Lonny asked. "Want to have dinner at a fish restaurant down on the wharf and come home early?"

"Home early and to bed?" I teased.

"That's right."

"You've got a deal."